BAD TO THE BONE

***Also by Jack Bodine
in Large Print:***

Beginner's Luck
The Reckoning
Apache Moon
Outlaw Hell
Devil's Creek Massacre

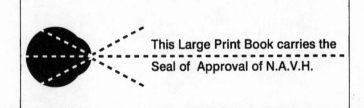

This Large Print Book carries the
Seal of Approval of N.A.V.H.

THE
PECOS KID
#6

BAD TO THE BONE

JACK BODINE

Thorndike Press • Waterville, Maine

Published in 2003 by arrangement with Lowenstein Associates, Inc.

Thorndike Press® Large Print Western Series.

The tree indicium is a trademark of Thorndike Press.

The text of this Large Print edition is unabridged. Other aspects of the book may vary from the original edition.

Set in 16 pt. Plantin.

Printed in the United States on permanent paper.

Library of Congress Cataloging-in-Publication Data

Bodine, Jack.
    Bad to the bone / Jack Bodine.
        p. cm. — (The Pecos kid)
    ISBN 0-7862-3860-7 (lg. print : hc : alk. paper)
    1. Braddock, Duane (Fictitious character) — Fiction.
2. Large type books. I. Title.
PS3552.O366 B39 2003
    813′.54—dc21   2001058470

BAD TO THE BONE

Duane Braddock leaned forward on his saddle, as a Mexican village twinkled in desert wastes straight ahead. He wasn't sure of its name, but had been travelling more or less toward Monterrey. He wondered whether to detour around the village, or stop at the cantina, have a glass of mescal, and maybe see some dancing girls.

Duane hadn't spoken to anybody except his horse for two weeks. He wasn't an American tourist or scholar, and didn't need a warm climate for his health. Duane Braddock, alias the Pecos Kid, was wanted for multiple murders in Texas.

It had been self-defense all the way, but he didn't trust crooked judges and rigged juries; the only law he respected was man-ufactured in Colonel Colt's factory in

Hartford, Connecticut. He brought his hand to rest on the comfortable grip of his .44 revolver. It made him feel safer in a land filled with banditos, warring revolutionaries, Comancheros, bears, and rattlesnakes.

The Pecos Kid wore black jeans, a green shirt, and a red paisley bandanna. On his head sat his black wide-brimmed cowboy hat held in place by a leather thong neckband. He was tall, slim, eighteen years old, hadn't shaved for several days, and looked like a strange, fearsome desert creature, which in a sense he was.

I should pass this place by, he reasoned, but it'd be nice to take a bath without worrying about an Apache shooting an arrow through my back. I'd have a plate of enchiladas, take a sip of mescal, and cool my heels.

He could speak Spanish fluently, because he'd been raised in a monastery populated by Spanish-speaking priests and brothers. But he tended to get into trouble at drinking establishments, because certain men couldn't hold their liquor, and the first thing they wanted was to punch somebody though a window. Unfortunately, Duane had fallen into the line of fire more than once.

But a man can't hide from the world forever, he told himself. He was approximately two hundred miles south of the Rio Grande, and doubted that the Fourth Cavalry would follow that far. I'm sure that the Army has more important things to worry about than one alleged killer, he deliberated.

The Pecos Kid liked bright lights and good times, like any red-blooded Texan. Youthful curiosity exceeded self-preservation yet again, and he really wanted to see some dancing girls.

His horse plodded toward adobe huts nestled in the valley, as Duane made a solemn oath to himself. If anybody provokes me, I'll turn the other cheek, just as Christ said in the Bible. If somebody pushes me, I won't push back. And if I have to apologize for something I didn't do, so what?

The town was Zumarraga, named after the first Bishop of Mexico, Juan de Zumarraga. Hub of a vast ranching area, it boasted a stable, a general store, several cantinas, and numerous impoverished hovels.

A steepled Catholic church was the spiritual center of Zumarraga, and in a back

9

pew knelt twenty-one-year-old Doña Consuelo de Rebozo. She was the daughter of one wealthy landowner, and married to another, but that didn't provide immunity from sorrow. Her mother, Doña Migdalia de Vásquez, was dying from cancer, and Doña Consuelo had been in prayer nearly constantly for the past several months.

"Hail Mary, full of grace, the Lord is with thee," she whispered, fingering rosary beads, while at the main altar the choir rehearsed for Sunday Mass.

Doña Consuelo felt afraid, vulnerable, and bewildered. The inevitability of her mother's impending doom demoralized her profoundly, and sometimes she felt like dropping down and crying her eyes out.

But she was descended from the Spanish nobility, and understood her duties well. She arrived at the end of her rosary, crossed herself, and uttered the final prayer. Then she arose, and turned toward her vaquero bodyguards, who sat in the first pews of the church, waiting for her to finish devotions. Her husband, Don Carlos de Rebozo, would never permit her to leave the hacienda without protection.

The bodyguards treated her like valuable treasure, because one word could get them dismissed. But Doña Consuelo would never dismiss anybody, and looked the other way when one vaquero took a sip from his pocket flask, or another flirted with a female in the vicinity. The body-guards never dared flirt with her, of course, because they respected her position, piety and goodness, and feared the wrath of Don Carlos. She was their *princesa*, and they followed her like a pack of poodles as she made her way toward the door.

The church was low-ceilinged, constructed of adobe and wood, with tiny altars along the sides, where candles burned in front of gaudily painted plaster saints. The choir sang a Gregorian chant, and a shudder of religious passion passed through Doña Consuelo. She'd led a relatively blameless life, had studied the Bible assiduously, and had obeyed her parents even when they told her who to marry. All she wanted was her own little baby to raise and love, but unfortunately she was barren after three years of marriage.

Pedro, leader of her bodyguards, rushed to the door and opened it. Doña Consuelo stepped into the moonlight, and the first thing she saw was a tall, slim Americano riding down the middle of the street, his face covered by his hat brim. Doña Consuelo paid no special attention as another of her bodyguards, Francisco, opened the door to her coach. She climbed inside, the carriage rolled out of Zumarraga, and Doña Consuelo gazed at businesses closed for the night, as pedestrians peered at the wealthiest woman in the territory. But she didn't take herself seriously, for priests had taught her the sin of false pride. All my maids have children, but not me, she reflected. Perhaps this will be the night I conceive.

The carriage came alongside the bearded, dusty, ragged Americano, who turned toward her suspiciously. Their eyes met. She saw a hunted animal, and shrank back into the carriage, wondering what terrible crime he had committed, because why else would he be so deep into *Mexico Lindo?* She felt grateful for her bodyguards, and wondered how ordinary women dared walk the streets of Zumarraga.

Doña Consuelo de Rebozo didn't see the fault line in her character, caused by overripe innocence, cramped opportunities, and narrow education. She hugged herself and smiled in the darkness, anticipating the strong arms of her husband, as the carriage rolled over the winding moonlit trail.

★ ★ ★

Duane Braddock rode down the center of the town, struck by the beauty of the woman he'd just seen. She'd had big brown eyes, a straight, perfectly chiseled nose, and petulant, pouting lips that begged to be kissed. Must be some rich man's wife, he decided, as he searched both sides of the street.

He passed the church, a variety of stores closed for the night, and lamps shining in the windows of jacales. Gregorian chants echoed down the street, but Duane tried not to hum the melodies. An old cowpoke had told him to study a town before he climbed off his horse, because nobody wants to blunder into danger. It looked like a sizable settlement, in the real Mexico where Americans seldom came.

Duane maintained his hand close to Colonel Colt's invention as he came to a two-story hotel with a wide veranda, where gentlemen and ladies sat with food and drink. Duane was tempted to join them, but knew he wouldn't feel comfortable without a wall to his back.

He glanced at rooftops, to make sure nobody was taking a bead on him, and hoped no American bounty hunters were in town, because they'd shoot him on sight

13

like a rabid dog. I should keep riding onward, but I have to stop sooner or later, he persuaded himself. What the hell — a man can't live on the desert forever.

The road narrowed into a neighborhood of shacks, huts, and vaqueros strolling the sidewalks, wearing long, flowing mustaches, gaudy bandannas, and immense sombreros. I must appear outlandish to them, speculated Duane, stroking his beard. I should shave but leave the mustache, and buy a sombrero and a pair of pants with stitching down the sides, with wide bottoms. When he'd lived in Texas, Mexicans had been the foreigners, but now the shoe was on the other hoof.

He rode through the town, then turned around and headed back, his eyes probing shadows, rooftops, and darkened alleyways. He noted the location of the calaboose, the bank, and the gun shop. Following his natural instincts, he found himself headed once more toward the cantina district. Hungry, thirsty, and lonely, he inclined his big black horse toward a complex of adobe huts that had no sign above the door. He climbed down from the saddle, threw the reins over the hitching rail, and gazed into the animal's luminous eyes.

Duane had "borrowed" him from an outlaw band farther north, and named him Midnight. He didn't know much about Midnight's history, but figured he'd been stolen somewhere along the way, which gave Duane something else to worry about.

"I'm going to have a drink," Duane explained, "but I shouldn't be long. If anybody tries to steal you, kick him in the ass. We'll probably spend the night on the desert, so enjoy yourself while you can."

Midnight plunged his snout into the water trough, as Duane loosened the two cinches beneath the saddle. Duane tried to treat Midnight as a friend, rather than mere transportation, but Midnight didn't seem to like him much. The Pecos Kid tossed his saddlebags over his shoulder, headed for the front door of the cantina, never letting his right hand stray from his Colt. He opened the door, and saw three drunkards sitting at a table in front of him. "Look at the gringo," said one of them.

Their glassy eyes probed as he retreated into the shadows. Ahead were tables and chairs all the way to the end of the large enclosed space. The bar was to the left, three deep with vaqueros, and every table was taken. Duane realized it must be Saturday night, of all times to come to town, but he wasn't about to ride away after just arriving.

He couldn't get close to the bar, but he noticed an empty length of wall between two vaqueros and backed into it. Waitresses and prostitutes in low-cut gowns moved among the crowd, sitting on men's laps or accompanying them to and from back rooms, while candles burned merrily on tables, casting dancing shadows on adobe walls. Above the bar hung a poster showing a naked blond lady reclining on a sofa covered with leopard skin.

A waitress passed, and Duane called out: "Señorita — would you bring a glass of mescal?"

She stared at him for a few moments, as if seeing him for the first time, "You are a long way from home, eh Americano?"

"I am very thirsty, if you do not mind."

She raised her right eyebrow skeptically, then headed for the bar. Meanwhile, on a small stage at the rear of the establishment, a vaquero strummed his flamenco guitar. Duane was struck by how similar the cantina was to the average Texas saloon; only the tune was different.

The waitress returned with the mescal, and he tossed her a few coins, tipping her extravagantly. "What's the name of this town?" he asked.

"Zumarraga."

"*Gracias,*" he said, bowing slightly, anxious to be polite, so as not to offend anybody.

She continued to look askance at him, as if he wasn't deceiving her. "What are you doing here, Americano?"

"I needed a drink." He tossed down the remainder of the mescal, placed his empty glass on her tray, and wanted to say *hit me again,* but a terrible conflagration had broken out in his chest. He swallowed hard, and his face turned red. The waitress walked away laughing.

Duane raised his hand to his mouth and broke into paroxysms of coughing. The mescal had gone down the wrong tube, and nearby Mexicans chuckled at his distress. I'm making a fool of myself, and holding Texas up to ridicule, he thought. Why do I constantly feel the need to show off in front of women, even ones I don't even give a damn about?

The musician wailed a sad song, and Duane could hear the pure romance of his wild vaquero life. Duane had been a cowboy once, and dreamed that he'd have his own ranch someday, raising his own family, after the law left him alone.

He began to feel a happy glow, as mescal filtered through his bloodstream. He loved the beverage because it produced interesting hallucinations, and the former acolyte enjoyed reflecting upon theology, morality, lost worlds, and the wisdom of the ages. What does it all mean, and why should I care? he asked himself, as the waitress returned with his next glass of mescal. Duane again tipped her abundantly, then raised his glass in a toast. "To Mexico," he said.

"What crimes are you wanted for?" she replied.

"What makes you think I'm wanted for crimes?"

"Why else would you be in Mexico?"

"My doctor said the climate is good for my heart."

"You do not seem sick to me, and you are not bad looking either . . . for an Americano." She fluttered her eyelashes. "Want to go upstairs?"

"Not today."

"What is wrong with today?"

He felt himself becoming nervous, because he didn't want to offend her. "I'm in love with somebody else."

"Where is she?"

"Far away."

"I'm right here, and I will love you with all my heart."

"I don't have much money."

"Too bad." She gave her shoulder a toss. "Perhaps some other time."

She walked away saucily, as Duane noticed vaqueros at the bar looking at him and talking earnestly, as if planning a necktie party. The troubadour continued to warble about romance till the end of time, as additional mescal poured into Duane's bloodstream. The cantina took on an orange haze. He saw the flush of men's faces as they played cards, while waitresses and prostitutes sashayed past, casting sultry glances, and lamplight pulsated everywhere.

Fermented maguey juice flowed through Duane's brain, as he felt the strange rhythms of Mexico pounding within him. Mayan priests, Spanish conquistadors, and armies of Catholic missionaries shimmered before him in the huge, unlikely cantina.

Duane had studied Mexican history at the monastery, and remembered a few facts. During the late 1850s, Mexico had defaulted on European loans, and soon endured invasion by France, England, and Spain. France had become dominant in the coalition, defeated the Mexican Army, and Napoleon III had installed an Austrian duke named Maximilian of Hapsburg as emperor of Mexico, with Maximilian's wife, Carlota, as his empress. They had ruled until 1867, when Mexican patriots under Benito Juárez had placed Maximilian before a firing squad. Empress Carlota had then booked passage on the next boat to Europe, where she subsequently went mad. Juárez was still president in early 1872, but large regions were dominated by banditos, Apaches, and wealthy caudillos who held the power of life and death over hundreds and sometimes thousands of peasants.

As Duane drained the glass and looked for the waitress, the door opened, and another gringo entered the cantina. He was approximately six-foot-two, his wide-brimmed silverbelly cowboy hat on the back of his head, and curly blond hair spilled down his forehead. He took one look at the crowd around the bar, hesitated, and backed out of the cantina.

Now there's a cautious man, figured Duane. Whoever he is, he's not looking for trouble, while I blithely walked in here, drank two glasses of mescal, and now my head is spinning. I've got to eat something, otherwise I'll pass out.

All the tables were taken. A different waitress walked by, and he placed his empty glass on her tray. He wanted to ask for a restaurant recommendation, but was afraid to open his mouth.

A vaquero and a woman entered the cantina as Duane headed for the door. The woman had wavy black hair, wide hips, and the vaquero's hand protecting the small of her back. As Duane drew closer, he became increasingly astonished by the sheer size of the woman's bosom. They must be awful heavy for her to carry around, he mused.

"What are you looking at!" demanded an angry voice.

The vaquero stared at Duane with undisguised rancor, and Duane realized too late that he'd been staring at the Mexican woman's breasts like a lecherous fool. The Americano smiled weakly. "I am sorry, señor, but I have drunk too much mescal, and I was on my way out of here."

"I saw you flirting with her," the vaquero said angrily. "You do not fool me."

All eyes in the vicinity turned toward the confrontation near the door. "I meant no insult to you or your woman," replied Duane. "It was a mistake."

The vaquero was four inches shorter

21

than Duane, but with larger shoulders, a barrel chest, and thick arms. "It was no mistake, because I saw your shameless eyes."

He's drunk, Duane realized, as he wondered how to extricate himself from the situation into which he was sinking. "I was looking at her, but you should take it as a compliment. She is, after all, a beautiful woman."

The woman smiled broadly, while the vaquero noticed her response with dismay. Duane realized that he'd said the wrong thing again, as the vaquero raised both fists to the fighting stance. He's not going to punch me, is he? wondered Duane. The vaquero cocked his left fist and threw it toward Duane's head, but Duane timed it coming in, and easily ducked beneath it. Then he took a few steps backward, as the crowd coalesced around them. It appeared that the entertainment had arrived.

The big-bosomed woman turned toward her vaquero and said reproachfully: "Leave him alone, Pablo. He is just a boy, and he meant no harm."

"He does not look like a boy to me," Pablo replied, his eyes bloodshot from excessive mescal. "Do you like him?"

"I do not know him — how could I like him?"

"I saw the way you were looking at him, and he was looking at you!"

The woman became pale. "But Pablo, it does not mean anything. You are always so suspicious."

A fiendish gleam came to Pablo's eyes. "I asked you — do you like him?"

"But you know that I love you!"

"I do not know any such thing, the way you flirt with men all the time. I'll show you what I do to men who look at you, and then maybe you will never flirt again." Pablo turned toward Duane, raised his fists, and advanced with mayhem in his eyes.

Duane backstepped, holding his hands down to his sides, not wanting to provoke anybody. "Now just a minute — let's not —"

Duane was unable to finish the sentence, because a big, hairy fist was zooming toward his very nose. He dodged to the side, the fist whizzed harmlessly by, and Duane was on his way toward the door. But vaqueros and prostitutes were crowded around, there was no clear path, and Pablo darted nimbly to cut him off.

Duane was the only gringo in the

cantina, and he wanted to avoid show-downs. He steadied himself, turned toward Pablo, and said: "If I've offended you in any way, I apologize from the bottom of my heart. I promise never, under any circumstances, to do it again."

Pablo responded with a right toward Duane's mouth, but Duane danced away lightly, still holding his hands down his sides. I've apologized from the bottom of my heart, I promised never to do it again, and if that's not good enough for this son-of-a-bitch, I guess I'll have to fight him.

But Duane realized he was in no condition to fight, as Pablo squared off again. The lone gringo was half drunk on an empty stomach, but adrenaline kicked in like a horse, causing his right leg to tremble, always the signal that he was getting into his fighting mode.

"Señor Pablo," Duane intoned carefully, "I'm going to tell you one last time. If you don't leave me alone, I'm going to start punching back. I don't know what the outcome will be, and maybe you'll kill me, but I promise you one thing, if you continue to press me, you will regret it."

The swarthy Mexican launched a long, looping overhand right at Duane's skull. Duane snatched his opponent's wrist out of the air, spun sharply, and threw him over his shoulder. The Mexican went flying over the bar, and crashed against the row of bottles beneath the mirror. Meanwhile, Duane headed for the door, and vaqueros in wide-brimmed sombreros made way. He reached the hitching rail, where Midnight dozed among other horses. "Wake up," Duane said. "We're in trouble again."

Duane tossed the saddlebags over Midnight's ebony haunches, then kneeled and tightened the two cinches beneath Midnight's massive belly. He untied the reins from the hitching rail, and was placing his foot into the stirrup, when the door of the cantina opened and Pablo appeared on the dirt sidewalk. "Not so fast, gringo!"

Vaqueros and their women crowded out the door to see the next installment of the fight. Duane wanted to jump onto Midnight and ride the hell out of there, but feared getting shot out of the saddle.

"Were you trying to sneak away?" asked Pablo, gazing malevolently at Duane. Pablo had cut the side of his head on a broken bottle, and blood oozed into his thickly matted hair, as his sombrero hung on leather thongs down his back.

"You shouldn't have followed me,"

replied Duane, "but you won't listen to reason."

The Mexican lunged toward Duane, who was standing between Midnight and a strange horse, leaving little room to maneuver. Duane tossed a short right jab to Pablo's nose and it connected on target, but the Mexican kept coming. He grabbed at Duane's throat, but Duane took a handful of Pablo's hair, pushed his head into the muck, leapt over him, and landed in the middle of the street.

Pablo growled as he arose, covered with mud and manure, stinking to high heaven. Meanwhile, a larger crowd was forming, and Duane spotted the blond American outlaw hanging in the shadows, watching the show. Pablo lowered his head, then charged Duane, flinging a wild hook at Duane's head, but Duane caught Pablo's wrist, pivoted, and let Pablo's forward movement carry him over Duane's shoulder.

The Mexican dropped onto the ground, rolled over, and came up with a knife in his hand. "I am going to kill you, gringo!" he screamed.

Moonbeams rolled along the seven-inch blade, and Duane took a step backward, for a knife raised the ante drastically.

"Whoa," he said to the Mexican. "Are you sure you want to *die* over something that I've already apologized for?"

"You are the one who is going to die!"

Pablo charged, slashing the blade toward Duane's face, but Duane darted to the side and stuck out his foot. The Mexican tripped over Duane's ankle, and landed on his face. This time he didn't get up so quickly.

Duane decided that the time had come to appeal to the common sense of the crowd. "Señores and señoritas," he declaimed, "if this man doesn't stop attacking me, I will kill him, or he will kill me. Doesn't he have a friend who can talk him out of it?"

Nobody stepped forward, especially not the woman with large breasts at the edge of the crowd. It appeared that everybody was afraid of Pablo, who was raising himself off the ground, the knife in his fist. "What is wrong, gringo?" he asked. "Are you afraid to stand still and fight?"

"Because I looked at your woman?" asked Duane. "You're acting like a fool."

Duane regretted the words the moment they'd left his mouth, but his nerves were jangled after three weeks in the saddle. Meanwhile, Pablo set his lips in a grim line, as his eyes narrowed for his next attack.

"Señor," said Duane. "If you come at me once more, I'm going to cut you, so help me God."

The Mexican got low and waved his blade from side to side menacingly. "Say your prayers, gringo."

Duane pulled his Apache knife out of his boot. It had a ten-inch blade crowned with a bear bone handle. He'd lived among Apaches for a spell, and they'd taught him the niceties of close combat with knives, rocks, fists, and anything else that might come to hand. He poised on the balls of his feet, when the Mexican suddenly stopped, feinted to the left, sidestepped to the right, and thrust his knife up suddenly, its point streaking toward Duane's belly.

Duane caught the Mexican's wrist in his left hand, stopping it cold, while stepping forward and touching the point of his knife to his adversary's throat. The iron point poked through Pablo's skin, and a dot of ruby red blood appeared.

"Drop the knife," said Duane.

The blade stung Pablo, and it wouldn't take much to puncture his jugular. His fingers loosened, as his weapon fell at Duane's feet.

"Señor Pablo," Duane told him, "if you ever come near me again — you're dead meat. Do you understand?"

Pablo sweated profusely, as blood trickled down his throat and made a blotch on his white shirt.

"And don't think," Duane continued, "that you'll sneak behind me someday, because I've got sharp ears, I shoot first, and ask questions later."

Pablo couldn't understand what had happened to him. He usually defeated other people easily, although he never picked fights with bigger men, of course.

"I asked you a question," Duane said, sticking his knife in another sixteenth of an inch.

"I understand," croaked Pablo reluctantly.

Duane heard footsteps behind him, and thought he was under attack. He withdrew his knife, spun around, and saw an astonishing figure at the edge of the crowd. The newcomer was taller than Duane, and wore a black leather jacket, ruffled white shirt, and silver conchos stitched down the seams of his black wide-bottomed trousers. He had silver hair and a silver mustache, and Duane pegged his age at the mid-fifties. "What is going on here!" he demanded.

A vaquero approached the personage and bowed. "Don Carlos, there was a fight. Pablo pulled a knife on that Americano, and the Americano nearly killed him."

Don Carlos's eyes flashed wry amusement, as he turned toward Pablo, who held his fingers to the puncture wound at his throat. "So you have been fighting again, eh?"

"The gringo has insulted my woman," Pablo replied. "He was trying to steal her from me." The vaquero looked like a hurt little boy who'd just lost his mommy.

Don Carlos turned toward Duane. "What is your side of the story?"

"I was on my way to a restaurant, and happened to look at his woman. It was not an incident worth fighting over."

Pablo's eyes bounced about excitedly. "My woman is not worth fighting over?"

Don Carlos chuckled. "Come now, Pablo. You are always angry about something, and maybe you are more trouble than you are worth. Go back to the hacienda, and I will speak with you later." Don Carlos placed one hand on his hip and glanced among the assembled vaqueros. "Has anyone seen my wife?"

A vaquero bowed. "She left the church a

half-hour ago, sir."

He must be the richest caudillo in the province, Duane thought. The Mexican nobleman had the physique of a young man, with a narrow waist and flat stomach. Just goes to show you that a cowboy doesn't have to get old when he's old, thought Duane.

Don Carlos ambled away, surrounded by his vaquero bodyguard. The woman with large breasts pulled a handkerchief from within her bosom, and wiped blood from Pablo's throat. *"Querido mío,"* she said tenderly, you must be loco, and perhaps that is why I love you so."

Duane scratched his head in confusion as they walked off arm in arm. He became aware of a short, pudgy Mexican standing beside him. "I am Fernando, and you are one fast son-of-a-bitch with a knife. Are you part Apache?"

"That's right," replied Duane. "What about you?"

"I work for Don Carlos, and when I look at a woman, nobody gives a damn."

"I wonder what women see in men like Pablo?"

Fernando showed the palms of his hands. "Nobody has ever explained love, señor."

"I'm hungry — do you know of a good

restaurant? I'd be happy to buy you supper."

Fernando led Duane into an alley, as vaqueros in the street mumbled amongst themselves. Duane touched his fingers to the grip of his Colt as he searched the shadows for a bushwhacker. He knew he should get out of Zumarraga immediately, but was tempted by the notion of a good hot meal.

"What can you tell me about Don Carlos?" asked Duane, as they crossed the backyard.

"He owns this town and all the land around here for miles and miles." Fernando winked as he waddled on his stubby legs. "And he has a pretty young wife."

"Where did he come from?"

"His family has always been here, señor. He is descended from an officer in the army of Hernán Cortés."

Cortés was the conqueror of Mexico, a hero to his Spanish descendants, but not loved by the Indians. Duane and Fernando approached a rectangular adobe hut with bright lights in the windows. Fernando opened the door. Men and women were seated at tables in a crowded space redolent with the fragrances of tobacco, mescal, and chili peppers.

Duane selected an empty table against the far wall, sat facing the door, and rolled a cigarette. Fernando motioned to the waitress. "I want a bowl of chili and a steak."

Duane noticed a face in the window, and it belonged to the blond American whom he'd seen earlier in the cantina. Now there's a man who knows what he's about, deduced Duane. I wonder who he is? The waitress was looking at Duane expectantly. "Bring me a plate of enchiladas," Duane told her, "and do you have mescal?"

The waitress headed for the kitchen as Duane lit his cigarette. He noticed everyone glancing at him cautiously, or staring in undisguised curiosity. "It's no fun," he said to Fernando, "living in a country where people don't like Americanos."

"Well, your country has stolen a substantial portion of this one."

"But I wasn't even alive then!"

"Do you think America should give Texas back?"

Duane decided to change the subject. "What do you think of President Juárez?"

"He is a great man," declared Fernando, "and he will make Mexico a great nation."

Duane puffed his cigarette as he examined the other denizens of the restaurant, many of whom were casting glances in his direction. I'll eat my meal, then hit the trail, he determined. One of these Mexicans is liable to kill me if I stay in this village much longer.

CHAPTER 2

Doña Consuelo de Rebozo sat at the end of her long dining room table, picking at roast chicken, stewed yams, and fried bananas. A silver rococo candelabra provided illumination, while a uniformed butler stood alertly in the shadows, awaiting her next request.

Doña Consuelo had been attended by servants all her life, and considered them part of the decor. She gave them presents and gifts of money whenever the mood struck her, and if they stole pieces of silverware and articles of jewelry from time to time, far be it from her to make a fuss. Her husband could afford it, and she wasn't there to judge anybody. Doña Consuelo wouldn't say boo to a goose.

She looked at the big grandfather clock against the wall, and wondered when Don

Carlos would return. She missed his commanding presence, ringing laughter, and the clever remarks that he always made. He never failed to light up a room, he was the finest man she'd ever known, finer even than her father. It gave her comfort to know that Don Carlos de Rebozo was all hers till death them did part, according to vows they'd taken before Holy Mother Church.

She hoped she didn't have to sleep alone that night, because she needed him more than usual, in the way a healthy woman sometimes needs a man. The butler, whose name was Alfonso, approached from the shadows and bowed reverently. "Would you like me to have your meal reheated, Doña Consuelo?"

"I'm finished, and you may take it away."

"Coffee?"

"No, thank you, and I don't want dessert. But leave the wine."

"As you wish, Doña Consuelo." With deft hands, Alfonso cleared the table of everything except bottle and glass. He retreated toward the kitchen, leaving Doña Consuelo alone in the dining hall.

Portraits of Don Carlos's illustrious ancestors stared down at her from the walls, while a suit of conquistador armor stood in the corner, helmet attached, and holding a lance. Doña Consuelo felt honored, ennobled, and glorified to be married to one of Mexico's most illustrious families, but if she didn't produce a son soon, God only knew the result.

Don Carlos didn't want a distant relative to inherit the Rebozo holdings when he died. No, he wanted a son of his own, but his first wife had been sickly, had failed to produce a child, and died from cholera. Don Carlos had mourned her death ten years, refusing to touch another woman, but then, at the urging of family members, he'd agreed to consider a girl of good family as second wife.

The most beautiful women in Mexico had been paraded before Don Carlos's discriminating eyes, sometimes at dinner parties in private homes, other times at receptions in government palaces. Doña Consuelo would never forget the instant she'd first set eyes on Don Carlos de Rebozo. She'd heard of him, of course, for his family's lineage was even older than hers, but she'd expected a bald, wrinkled, and portly gentleman with teeth missing and tobacco juice on his mustache. Instead, Don Carlos de Rebozo had looked like El Cid in his immaculately tailored suit. They'd met at a reception for the governor at her uncle's mansion in Durango, and she'd been struck by Don Carlos's slender figure, full head of hair, and the intelligent glint in his eye.

She'd thought such a man could never love a silly young thing such as herself, without a brain in her head, and possessing no skills for managing a household. Yet she knew that she was considered pretty, though she suspected not as pretty as most of the young ladies in attendance. The concept of flirting was repugnant to her sequestered religious nature.

"Walk past him," her mother had suggested. "You must show yourself to your best advantage."

"You sound as if you're selling a horse," replied Consuelo. "If he wants to look at me, let him come over here."

As her mother fretted, Consuelo had sat in a plushly upholstered chair in a corner and watched, with smoldering eyes, as Don Carlos de Rebozo worked his way across the room. Finally he came to a stop in front of her, and her mother bowed low, making the proper introductions.

"How do you do," said Don Carlos to young Consuelo, in the tones of an educated man.

She curtsied before him. "My mother has been talking about nothing but you for weeks, sir. I'm proud to meet the most ostentatiously eligible man in Mexico."

Her mother nearly fainted, and a flicker of amusement passed over the great man's tanned visage. "And I'm honored to meet such a splendid señorita. But tell me, my dear, why are you hiding in the corner?"

"Hiding?" She looked from side to side. "Do I appear to be hiding? Just because I have not thrown myself at Don Carlos de Rebozo, like all the other señoritas, does that mean I am hiding?"

A maid administered smelling salts to Consuelo's mother as Don Carlos took a step backward and looked Consuelo up and down. "May I call on you this Saturday afternoon?"

"That would give me great pleasure, sir," she replied, "but you must ask my mother's permission first. However, since she has fainted dead away, I will answer for her and say *yes*."

And thus had begun their great love. She reflected upon it warmly as she made her way down the long lantern-lit corridor to the master bedroom. Many of the distinguished individuals whose portraits graced the walls had attended her wedding, while she had been center of the extravagant production, with everyone acting his or her designated role — and with the celebrated Don Carlos de Rebozo as her leading man. Since childhood, she'd dreamed of marrying a prince, and her wedding had been the fulfillment of that noble childhood aspiration.

Her wedding night had satisfied her hidden and less noble desires. She'd never admit it, not even to her mother, but as a young girl she'd frequently fantasized the most disturbing and unsettling desires concerning males. Often she'd suffered dreams where she'd awakened panting, covered with sweat. It wasn't a subject that a young girl could discuss with her priest, but she knew darkly and dimly that marriage could provide a possible solution to the problem.

She undressed in front of the mirror, her body illuminated by a candelabra on the dresser that reflected off mirrors, providing golden effulgence. She'd gained weight since getting married, but that was considered appropriate for Mexican ladies. In another two or three years, at the rate she was going, they'd call her pleasingly plump, but at present she still was a smooth-limbed, healthy-looking woman with full breasts, firm muscles, and a certain naughty gleam that occasionally came to her eyes.

She dropped a light silk gown over her shoulders, then knelt at the foot of her bed, crossed herself, and prayed for the safety of her husband, the health of her mother, and all the usual items, recrossing herself, and crawled into bed.

The white cotton sheets warmed with her body heat, but she felt lonely. Where is he? she wondered, as she lay frustrated in the darkness. Meanwhile, a maid tiptoed silently around the room, blowing out the candles. Doña Consuelo rolled onto her stomach and tried to get comfortable, as she remembered her wedding night.

She'd been half-terrified and half-lustful as she'd undressed in the dark with her husband. Then she'd lain stark naked on the bed, her heart beating wildly, alone with a man for the first time in her life.

The great caudillo had knelt between her legs and performed a certain act that she'd never imagined possible, and then, when she was completely relaxed, he'd made her into a real woman, stoking her fires until she shrieked with passion and madness. Needless to say, marriage to Don Carlos had soothed her worst frustrations, and she couldn't imagine being with anybody else.

Where in the name of God is he? she wondered, as she tossed and turned on her wide mattress. Doesn't he know how much I need him?

The stream was black ink flecked with silver, as Duane glanced about, listened, and waited, because Apaches liked to bushwhack lost wandering White Eyes near water.

He climbed down from the saddle, sat on the riverbank, and listened to the music of the night. Midnight grazed and watered himself, as Duane scanned cholla and nopal cactus for signs of Apaches on the prowl. He wished for a refuge where he didn't need to glance over his shoulder every few minutes, but no matter where he went, town or the open desert, he had to watch his ass.

He wished he could light a cigarette, but there was no smoking in Apache territory. Sometimes he longed for a woman, although he knew women generally led to trouble, such as the fight in Zumarraga. Sometimes Duane felt like jumping out of his skin and screaming at the top of his lungs. He felt hemmed in by life, constantly under assault, frustrated, confused, and bewildered.

Yet, paradoxically, he also felt invincible, overconfident, and optimistic about the future, the result of being young and filled with energies he couldn't control. He heard no sounds of an unshod hoof against the ground, or the measured moccasin tread of an Apache, so he undressed quickly, withdrew a sliver of soap from his saddlebag, and waded into the cold water.

It was deep as his waist, with smooth rocks on the bottom and the full moon shining in the sky. Teeth chattering, he soaped himself quickly, pausing occasionally to listen, his Colt lying on a boulder three feet away. He shampooed his hair, dived beneath the surface, shook off the dirt, and headed for shore.

He put on his last clean clothes: black jeans, black shirt, and yellow bandanna. Climbing onto Midnight, he urged the animal across the stream. Midnight's hooves splashed through the water as he headed toward a dark canyon in the distance. Duane pulled his hat tightly onto his wet head and searched for a lonely out-of-the-way spot to spend the night.

Doña Consuelo opened her eyes with a start as her husband entered the darkened bedroom. He wore his black velvet robe, for he'd bathed before coming to her.

"Where have you been?" she asked, raising her head from the bed.

"Business," he replied, gruffly.

He never explained anything to her, because he didn't think she understood. Don Carlos considered his wife a beautiful but naive young work of art with whom he had the good fortune to be married. He removed his robe in the darkness, because he didn't want her to see his aged wrinkled nakedness without benefit of the girdle he wore beneath his suits.

Unrestrained, his belly protruded like that of any gentleman in his fifties who tended toward overindulgence in food and drink. He crawled into bed, bussed her cheek, and said, "I'm awfully tired, and I really must get some sleep."

He rolled over, wheezed, and closed his eyes. She gazed at his noble profile outlined by light streaming through the windows, and felt guilty about her womanly requirements. Don Carlos de Rebozo had more important things to do than play with his giddy little wife.

Besides, Doña Consuelo was sleepy herself, having just been awakened from a vague dream. Certainly there are drawbacks to being married to an older man, she mused, but when he's awake and feeling strong, I'll bet he's a better lover than any young man.

Doña Consuelo had no way of knowing this, for she'd been a virgin prior to her marriage, and would never dream of being unfaithful to her beloved husband. But she believed it anyway, just as she believed in the transubstantiation of sacramental wine into the Most Precious Blood, or the Immaculate Conception. She snuggled against her bewhiskered husband, and dropped back to troubled sleep, hoping that he'd feel better tomorrow night, or possibly the night after.

Duane found a level length of ground alongside a seepweed bush, and decided it would be his bed for the night. Far from main trails, at the edge of a vast basin, it was possible that no white man had ever been in the vicinity since the dawn of time.

He unsaddled Midnight, picketed him, and laid out the bedroll. Then he crawled inside, using his saddle for a pillow, with his Winchester rifle lying nearby. He rolled onto his back and stared at the heavens filled with swirling stars.

Duane was tired of the owlhoot trail, and

wished he could lead a normal life. He knew that many wanted men changed their names, moved to another part of Texas, and no one knew who they were. That was his master plan, but there was something he had to do first.

Duane harbored a dark secret of which he was greatly ashamed. His parents had never married, and then they'd been murdered when he was one year old. According to information that he'd uncovered, his father, Joe Braddock, had been a rancher sucked into a range war with a big money man named Sam Archer of Edgeville, Texas. Duane's mother had been Miss Kathleen O'Shea, daughter of another small rancher. Joe Braddock and his gang, known as the Polka Dots, had been hunted by Sam Archer's paid killers, and massacred somewhere in Mexico. Shortly thereafter, Duane's mother had died of illness and grief, and Duane Braddock had been taken to the monastery that raised him.

Duane had hardly known his father, but vaguely remembered a hearty fellow with a thick black mustache, carrying the fragrance of whiskey, tobacco, and gunpowder. His mother had been blond, with frail features and a few freckles. According to what he'd been told, Miss Kathleen

O'Shea had been a devout Catholic, and when she was dying, had ordained that her baby son be sent to the monastery, so he could become a priest someday.

It hadn't worked that way, because Duane had got sick of the scriptorium less than a year ago. Since then he'd been on a quest to discover what had happened to his parents, and avenge their deaths. My mother and father fought for their rights against the big money combine from the East, he thought, but they were outnumbered, outgunned, and paid the ultimate price.

Duane had never met Sam Archer, didn't know what he looked like, but hated him anyway. "You think you've got away with the crime, Mister Rancher Man, but you're wrong," whispered Duane. "You can surround yourself with hired guns, but I lived with the Apaches, and I can outsmart any hired gun who ever lived. No matter how many miles I have to travel, or how many mountains must be climbed on my hands and knees, I'm going to track you down. You might be sleeping peacefully right now, but one day I'll put a bullet into your bean."

Duane wondered if he had the sand to calmly and deliberately shoot a man in the head, but he'd cross that bridge when he came to it. First he had to stay on the dodge awhile, until the Fourth Cavalry got tired of looking for him. Then he'd head for Edgeville, for his unscheduled meeting with Sam Archer.

Just a little while longer, then I'll be free to do whatever I want, Duane promised himself. When Mister Archer is buried in his grave, I'm going to be a cowboy again, and to hell with this cold and lonely owlhoot trail.

Doña Consuelo opened her eyes with a start, at the second knock on the door. "Who's there?"

The voice of García, her husband's foreman, came to her ears. "Something has happened! Is Don Carlos there?"

Doña Consuelo shook her husband firmly. "Wake up — Don Carlos!" she spoke urgently into her husband's hairy ear.

He grunted like an old buffalo as he opened his eyes. "What the hell is going on?"

"García is here — it's important!"

The great caudillo rolled out of bed slowly and with great difficulty. In the wan moonlight she could make out his rotund belly, not to mention his flaccid legs. He pulled the robe around his shoulders, opened the door, and disappeared into the corridor.

Consuelo wondered what had happened. It could have been an Indian raid on their cattle, a murder, illness, an accident, a fire, or any one of a thousand terrible calamities. She rolled over and wrapped her arms around her husband's pillow, inhaling his fragrance, and blushing at the mere thought of her physical needs.

The door opened, as Don Carlos returned to the bedroom. "I'm afraid it's your mother," he said. "She's taken a turn for the worse."

Consuelo's first reaction was that God was punishing her for her evil desires. "What happened?"

"She collapsed this afternoon, evidently. The doctor says that she won't last much longer."

Doña Consuelo sucked wind, "But . . . but . . ." She couldn't digest the news.

He placed his hand on her forehead. "My poor darling, I know how you love your dear mother. We'll leave for your father's hacienda first thing in the morning. Be calm, and pray to God for strength."

He sat with his arm around her shoulders, as she felt morbid terror arising from the floorboards of the bedroom. Her mother had nurtured, pampered, and taught her everything she knew. Without her mother, she'd be devastated, for her father had always been remote, and her husband had more important things to do than hold her hand and listen to her babble.

Doña Consuelo knew that cancer consumed people from the inside, sucking their lives away, causing them to die shriveled and ancient before their time. Tears flowed down her cheeks, as her husband sought to comfort her. "There, there," he cooed. "People live and die every day, but life goes on, and so shall we."

CHAPTER 3

Next morning, approximately two hundred miles to the north, a dusty stagecoach rolled down the main street of Escondido, a bustling town on the American side of the Rio Grande. No one paid special attention to the conveyance, because Escondido was the site of much trading activity, most of it illicit, between Texas and Mexico.

In the cab, among the other passengers, sat a tall blonde woman named Miss Vanessa Fontaine. She was dressed in a lavender mohair dress trimmed with blue velvet, with a white crepe de chine scarf. She gazed sullenly out the window at adobe buildings lining both sides of the street, and horse manure lying in the middle, along with whisky bottles, scraps of paper, bones of animals picked clean by dogs, and various other items too mis-shapen to recognize.

Miss Vanessa Fontaine was a lady of the world, and nothing fazed her, not even a filthy little border town. She pulled her head inside the window and looked at her fellow passengers: a cowboy, a lawyer, and a traveling salesman who'd been her company since Fort Stockton.

"It's not much," said the salesman, whose name was Charlie McPheeter, "but you'd be surprised the amount of traffic that passes through a town like this, and they all need hardware to replace somethin' that's broke. If yer innerested in money, it's a damn fine town, but if yer worried about a stray bullet a-flyin' over yer head, yer in the wrong damned place."

The lawyer replied: "Half the residents are wanted by the Mexican or American authorities, and as far as I know, there are no lawyers in Escondido. It's wide open for a fellow like me."

"We'll all be a-suein' each other inside of a week," drawled the drunken cowboy, who was sprawled in the corner, a bottle of something in his hand.

The lawyer sneered at the oafish fellow, but Vanessa considered the cowboy the most interesting passenger on the stagecoach, because he was exactly what he appeared to be, and made no bones about it.

The stagecoach came to a stop before a large hotel, and on the veranda, a vaquero with a cigar in his mouth strummed a guitar. Someone opened the coach door, and a wave of sundust entered the tiny enclosed cab. A hand grabbed Vanessa's wrist, and before she could do anything, it pulled her out the door.

"Howdy," said an American cowboy with a stubbled chin, his shirt unbuttoned to his waist. "You're just about the best-lookin' woman I've ever saw."

She looked at him reproachfully, and he released her, took a step backwards, and smiled unsteadily. "I meant no harm, miss. It's just that yer beauty bowled me —"

She turned away in the middle of his sentence as if he didn't exist. Atop the cab, the stagecoach guard threw down a bag to a gentleman in a green visor. Vanessa looked at the squat desert town while a crowd of beggars formed around the stage-coach. Men gazed at her from the sidewalk, her golden hair catching every ray of sun. "Can anyone help me with my bags?"

"Will I do?" asked her cowboy traveling

companion, whose name was Pyle. "I'm a-lookin' fer a job."

"Do you think you can carry those bags for me?"

"Yes ma'am," he winked lewdly, "and if thar's anythin' else you want, don't hesitate to ask."

She glanced at him skeptically. "Such as?"

"You know." He slowly ran his tongue across his upper lip.

"You drunkard — if you were ever alone with a woman, you wouldn't know the first thing to do. I'll see you in the lobby, and don't leave anything behind."

Everybody in the small, cramped chande-liered lobby stared as she crossed to the desk, where the young clerk, attired in a suit with a string tie, awaited her. "Ma'am?"

"I'd like the best suite of rooms in the hotel."

"We only have one kind of room, ma'am."

"Then I guess you'll have to knock down a few walls for me, because I need my elbow room. I am Miss Vanessa Fontaine, and perhaps you've heard of me."

"Who?"

Vanessa heard the voice of Pyle. "They

calls her the Charleston Nightingale, and she's supposed to be the best singer west of the Pecos."

The desk clerk vaguely remembered hearing something about a Charleston Nightingale who sang in saloons. "Yes ma'am, anythin' you say." He spun the register around. "Sign here."

Pyle admired her languid form as she bent over the desk and scratched her name with the quill pen. Then she strolled down the corridor, followed by her new servant carrying two suitcases in each hand, his tongue hanging out.

The room was far too small for Vanessa's tastes, with a window that opened on a corner of the backyard. The bed was graced with the customary cavern in the center, a dresser, and a wood chair. A scrap of Mexican blanket was nailed to the wall for decoration, and the narrow space carried the faint odor of whisky, tobacco, and men's sweat. She opened the window, pulled back the shades, and made way for the arrival of her suitcases.

"A real nice room," said Pyle, as he put the luggage down.

She handed him the coins. "Please stop leering, for God's sake. Why do you get so drunk?"

"What the hell else is there to do?"

He slammed the door on his way out, and she heard his footsteps recede down the hall. Then she untied her bonnet, hung it on the bedpost, removed her boots, stretched out on the plain blue bedspread, and stared at the ceiling. What have I done to myself this time? she asked herself.

Beneath her confident facade, she entertained serious doubts about the enterprise on which she was embarked. Her journey had begun approximately three months ago in Austin, and she was searching for a certain young man with whom she'd enjoyed an all-too-brief love affair. According to newspaper reports, Escondido was the last spot where he'd been seen.

Somehow, Duane Braddock continued to intrigue her, although she'd previously considered him far too young for her best interests. Miss Vanessa Fontaine was thirty-one, a former Charleston belle spoiled by a doting father. She'd survived the great Civil War by the skin of her teeth, and now was chasing an alleged outlaw across the Texas landscape, for reasons she didn't want to contemplate.

Duane Braddock wasn't her first love by any means. Her first beau had been killed in the War of Northern Aggression, and then there had been certain dalliances, for she'd surrendered to loneliness at certain low moments of her career. In retrospect, Duane had been her second true love, and the only one still alive, as far as she knew. She hadn't been able to forget him, although she'd dumped him in favor of an Army officer who'd subsequently been killed in action against the Apache.

I'll get a bath, and then go looking for Duane, she thought. If he's not in Escondido, I'll catch the next stage to Charleston, and start living like a person for a change. It's ridiculous to pursue a mere boy to the far ends of the frontier, especially since he probably hates me for jilting him. It's time I came to my senses and gave up this pointless and insane quest.

She often wondered why she couldn't forget Duane Braddock, but there'd been something decent and honorable about him; he was unlike the usual saloon rat that one encountered on the frontier. Sooner or later I'll tire of hunting for him, she acknowledged, but until then, I'd better get on with that bath.

Miss Vanessa Fontaine didn't fall in love every day, and she could no longer accept substitutes. Until something better came along, or she became bored, she intended to remain on Duane Braddock's trail.

Dozing in the saddle, Duane heard popping sounds in the distance. It sounded like a gun battle straight ahead. His first instinct was ride to the nearest hill and see what was going on, but then his Apache mind took over — Apaches believed in riding away from the sound of shots, not toward them.

Duane was immobilized by indecision yet again, while Midnight came to a halt, awaiting orders. It sounded like a small war, and the safe solution would be to take cover until the fighting blew over, but youthful curiosity won out yet again.

He spurred Midnight toward an eminence that might provide a view. Whatever it is, Duane warned himself, I'm not going to poke my big nose into it. The sun beat down on Duane, birds flitted among cactus and juniper trees, and something bit the back of his neck. He smacked the beetle with the palm of his hand, then flicked it away with his fingernail.

Midnight reached the summit, and Duane rested his forearm on his pommel as he leaned forward and studied the scene spread before him. It appeared that a stagecoach was running wild in the distance, its driver and guard shot by a gang of Mexican banditos who were still in hot pursuit, while other Mexicans on horseback tried to fight the banditos off.

Duane reached into his saddlebags and pulled out an old brass spyglass stamped C.S.A. He spit on the ends, polished them with his bandanna, and raised the instrument to his eye. The horses pulling the stagecoach appeared seriously spooked, and a woman was trapped inside the cab, which was in danger of tipping over.

Banditos and vaqueros fought a desperate running gun battle around the stagecoach, but a man can't aim straight on the hurricane deck of a horse. Duane trained the spyglass on the woman, and detected stark terror on her features. The stagecoach could strike the wrong rock at any moment, lose a wheel, and that would be the end of one Mexican señorita. Duane didn't even stop to think about it, but nudged his spurs into Midnight. "Let's go save her, boy."

Midnight loped down the rise, getting into the spirit of the chase. If there was anything he loved, it was running flat out with the bit loose in his teeth and not much weight on his spine. The horse accelerated as Duane tucked the spyglass into his belt, yanked his Colt, and crouched low like a jockey boy, presenting low resistance to the wind. He might be shot in the next few moments, but the Pecos Kid couldn't live with himself if he laid back while a woman got killed.

Midnight galloped at a right angle to the stagecoach, as Duane intended to cut it off farther along the trail. The banditos and the stagecoach defenders were heavily engaged, not paying any attention to the lone rider speeding across the desert. Volleys of fire echoed off sandstone cliffs, as banditos sought to break through the protective cordon around the stagecoach. Duane thought that it must be carrying gold, and that was why the banditos were trying to steal it.

Midnight burst through a thicket of paddle cactus, sharp needles tore Duane's jeans, and he came into view of the banditos and vaqueros. Wind flattened the front brim of Duane's hat as Midnight plunged onward, kicking up stones and clumps of grama grass. Duane leaned forward, working his body with the motions of Midnight, urging the horse to greater effort.

Midnight's hooves pounded the desert,

and shots whizzed around Duane as he came abreast of the carriage. He turned and found himself looking at a pale young woman with lustrous black hair and panic in her eyes. She appeared on the verge of apoplexy, so he winked reassurance, and said: "I'm going to stop those damned horses if I can."

Midnight pulled ahead steadily, a long lash of saliva escaping his lips. Duane holstered his gun as the big stagecoach wheel spun furiously a few feet away. The stagecoach driver lay dead in the boot, shot through the chest, while the shotgun guard was gone, and baggage bounced on the cage atop the coach.

Midnight gained on the sweating team of horses as Duane studied the complicated system of reins, harnesses, and traces. "Come on, boy," he whispered into Midnight's ear. "We've got to catch the nigh leader."

I know my job better than you, Midnight snorted, as he steeled himself for the final burst of speed. He'd come a long way, but so had the team of horses, and they were just nags as far as he was concerned. The black horse filled his great lungs with air and stretched his long limbs as he flew over the ground.

The thunder of massed hooves filled Duane's ears, along with the rattle and clank of the stagecoach at top speed. Duane glanced to the side and saw fire in the bloodshot eyes of the horses. "Hey — settle down!" he hollered at them, but only succeeded in frightening them further.

The air was filled with tumultuous sounds as Midnight rampaged onward, coming abreast of the nigh leader. "Just a little closer," Duane said, as he raised himself in his stirrups.

This is as close as I'm getting, Midnight seemed to reply. The horse's withers nearly touched the flanks of the nigh leader, as the team of horses roared over the winding trail. Duane took a deep breath, knowing he should've stayed in bed that morning, and raised his leg over the saddle, poised to leap onto the nigh leader.

Unfortunately, Midnight cut away when he felt the weight leave his back, upsetting Duane's aim. The Pecos Kid landed against the side of the lead horse, and hung on for dear life as his feet hit the trail. He kicked hard, bolted into the air, and this time overshot his mark, landing in the complicated tangle of traces and harnesses between the two lead horses. He was on the way to death by stomping, but managed to grab two fistfuls of leather straps, and hold himself steady.

He gazed at hooves churning up the trail, as the traces kicked and jolted him like a rag doll. Inches from death, he made one last superhuman effort, and climbed to the back of the nigh leader. Nearly deafened by hammering hooves, Duane hugged the animal's belly with his legs, grabbed the reins, and pulled back with all his might.

"Whoa!" he bellowed. "It's all right now!"

The nigh leader drew his great head back in distaste and shook his head, slowing his gait, impeding the progress of the other horses. Duane gritted his teeth as he struggled with the reins, but it appeared that he had them under control. Gradually the beasts slowed, their great chests heaving, as a cloud of dust swept forward, enveloping Duane.

He heard hoofbeats coming closer and didn't know if it was friend or foe, so he drew his Colt and thumbed back the hammer. The nigh leader came to a halt as a rider appeared through the swirling dust. It was a bandito aiming a pistol at Duane, and the Mexican fired first. Duane felt the warm slug pass his ear, then leveled his

Colt and fired at a range of five yards. The cartridge detonated, and a red dot appeared on the bandito's white shirt. His eyes rolled into his head as he dropped out of the saddle.

Duane jumped down from the nigh leader, ran to the cab, and opened the door. The Mexican woman cowered in the corner, aiming a shotgun at him. "One step closer," she said, lips quivering, "and I'll kill you."

"I'm here to help," Duane replied. "Who d'ya think just stopped this stagecoach?"

Before she could answer, Duane heard a horse behind him. He spun and saw another bandito barreling toward him, aiming a pistol at his head. Duane fired first and missed; then the Mexican shot his pistol, and lead slammed into the side of the stagecoach two inches from Duane's cheek. The bandito tried to smash Duane in the head with his gun barrel, but Duane grabbed the Mexican's wrist, twisted, and dragged him out of the saddle. The Mexican bounced on the ground and tried for another shot, but Duane beat him to the draw. Colonel Colt spoke his verdict, and the bandito's throat was pierced by a bullet.

Duane glanced toward the team of

skitterish horses, as they flinched beneath bullets whizzing in all directions. "Are you all right?" he asked the young woman.

"Watch out!" she screamed.

It was another rider charging through smoke and dust. Like the others, he aimed his gun at Duane, but Duane fired first, and the Mexican fell to the ground beside the carriage, a small hole in his forehead, and the back of his head blown off.

The Mexican woman turned a lighter shade of pale, and flopped backwards on the seat, her eyes going white. Duane crawled in with her and slapped her cheek lightly. "What's going on here?"

But she was out cold. He turned around, and saw that the banditos were riding away. He quickly reloaded his gun, as the woman came to consciousness behind him. "Who are you?" she asked in a sing-song voice.

"Just a drifter, and if I'm not mistaken, the banditos are headed for the hills."

She looked out the window as he stood to the side, admiring her profile. Isn't this the woman I saw in Zumarraga? "You are right," she said. "We have fought them off."

A vaquero rode toward them, his gun aiming straight up into the air. "It is

Pérez," she told Duane. "Don't shoot."

Pérez was covered with dust, and his left forearm bled profusely. "I think we had better return to the hacienda, Doña Consuelo. This is not a safe place to be."

Her eyes flashed, and Duane admired her pouting lips from the sidelines. "No place in Mexico is safe from banditos, but I must see my mother. We are continuing onward."

"But Doña Señora!"

"Direct your men to check the horses, and we might as well stop here for a meal."

"We cannot stop here, Doña Señora," Pérez said impatiently, "because we don't want the banditos to know where we are, in case they come back." Then he looked at Duane. "Who are you?"

"Just happened along."

"You are a very brave man, and you have saved Doña Señora's life. You'd better get that leg looked after."

"What leg?"

Duane looked down, and was surprised to see a bullet hole through the center of his thigh. Somehow, in the excitement, he hadn't even noticed it, nor did he know where it had come from. Suddenly it felt as if a flaming Aztec spear had been hurled through his flesh, and he gasped in pain.

"My God," he thought, as he noticed his pantleg soaked with blood. The wagon spun around him, along with a crowd of vaqueros, not to mention the petulant lips of the woman whose life he'd saved. He blacked out and fell in a clump to the ground.

In late afternoon, Miss Vanessa Fontaine strolled the sidewalks of Escondido, carrying her parasol, while her Spiller & Burr .36 revolver slept peacefully in the hand-tooled black leather holster held to her waist by a black leather gunbelt. Cowboys, outlaws, vaqueros, and horse thieves examined her like diamond merchants with fine gems, as her eyes fell on a sign:

SHERIFF

It hung over the sidewalk, and on the inside of the window was pasted:

J. T. STURGIS.

She entered the sheriff's office, where a man of twenty-nine sat at the desk, a badge pinned to his shirt. He was reading the stack of documents that had arrived on the recent stage. He glanced at Vanessa, shot to his feet, and a big grin spread over his face. He had brown hair, a mustache, and roving eyes. "What can I do fer you, ma'am?"

She stopped in front of his desk and looked him in the eyes. "One of this town's former sheriffs was a friend of mine, name of Duane Braddock. I'm looking for him."

"He ain't hyar," replied the sheriff. "You a friend of his'n?"

"Why else would I be asking about him? Do you know where he went?"

"The only person who could tell you that is Maggie O'Day."

Vanessa endured a bolt of jealousy, but maintained her perfect composure. "Who's Maggie O'Day?"

"She owns the best saloon in town, the Last Chance just down the street."

"Was she his lady friend?"

J. T. Sturgis held up the palms of his hands. "I wasn't here when Braddock was in town — don't ask me. When last seen, according to the Fourth Cavalry, he was a-ridin' hard toward Mexico." Sturgis winked. "How come a nice girl like you is a friend of the Pecos Kid?"

"If Duane Braddock ever shows up again, I hope you won't shoot first and ask questions later."

"Depends on him. Say, why don't you let me buy you dinner tonight at the Last Chance Saloon?"

"I'm busy."

"This is an awful dangerous town."

Vanessa pulled her Spiller & Burr and sighted down the barrel at the sheriff's nose. "I'm an awfully dangerous woman."

"That ain't loaded, is it?"

"It wouldn't make sense to carry it unloaded, would it?" With a smile, she holstered the weapon. "Don't worry, sheriff. I've never shot a lawman yet."

The line reverberated across the sheriff's walls, as Miss Vanessa Fontaine swooped toward the door. The sheriff blinked in disbelief as she was swallowed by the shimmering Texas afternoon. *She's a high-stepping filly, just the kind I like,* considered the sheriff. *I'm going to get into her pants if it's the last thing I do.*

Duane Braddock gradually came to full awareness. He was sprawled on his back in the rocking stagecoach, his leg a cylinder of pain, and he gazed at the profile of Doña Consuelo de Rebozo staring out the window at vast expanses of sunbaked desert.

Her shoulder-length black hair needed

combing, dust covered her Castilian features, and her skin was like fine Italian marble. She possessed a nearly perfect nose, without the hint of a bump in the middle, while her nostrils could have been carved by Michelangelo. Her high-buttoned silk blouse was decorated with crimson threads, and her skirt was golden brown brocade trimmed with side-pleated flounces. Unfortunately, she wore a rock the size of a robin's egg on her finger, which meant she belonged to another man. I wonder what it's like to sleep with a woman like that, mused Duane.

A soggy cloak of Catholic guilt dropped over him, as he caught his imagination *en flagrante* with a married lady. He blushed, tried to find a more comfortable position, and she turned toward him, her sensuous lips forming a friendly smile. "How are you feeling?" she inquired.

"I think I'm still alive. Where are we?"

"On the way to my father's hacienda, because my mother's very ill. We'll take care of you till you can walk, and I'd like to thank you for saving my life. You are a very courageous man. What's your name?"

"Just call me Duane."

"I am Doña Consuelo de Rebozo."

"What do your friends call you for short?"

She thought for a few moments. "I don't have any friends."

"How come?"

"I live in a remote place, and I guess you'd say my husband is my best friend, but most people call me Doña Consuelo."

"A beautiful name . . . for a beautiful woman."

She waved her hand impatiently. "You're delirious from loss of blood."

"What happened to my horse?"

"He is tethered to the back of the stagecoach."

With great effort, Duane poked his head out the window. Sure enough, Midnight lumbered along behind the coach, and Duane waved. "Thanks for the good work, feller."

Midnight nodded, the usual depressed expression on his face. He always seemed unhappy, although Duane tried hard to treat him well. Duane pulled his head back into the stagecoach, and saw Doña Consuelo looking at him curiously. "Do you frequently talk with your horse?" she asked.

"He's the most interesting conversationalist I know."

She couldn't help smiling, revealing straight white teeth like the finest ivory.

"Are you an American outlaw?"

He doubted that she was a Pinkerton man, bounty hunter, or U.S. marshal with a warrant for his arrest. "There are some people who think I've committed a few crimes, but it's not so."

"Whatever you've done, my husband will reward you for your bravery — and you're going to be a rich man. We have plenty of room at the hacienda, and I'm sure you can use a vacation. I owe my life to you, and if there's anything I can do to make you more comfortable, please don't hesitate to ask."

Vanessa Fontaine stood across the street from the Last Chance Saloon, wondering how to traverse the sea of mud, muck, manure, and something that looked like a dead bird. Escondido was without question the most disgusting town she'd ever seen. Across the street stood an immense saloon constructed of several adobe buildings jammed together behind a freshly painted false facade. A young harlot sat at a window on the second floor and knitted demurely, advertising the Last Chance Saloon as a whorehouse, while men passed back and forth between swinging batwing doors, trying to look up her dress. Absolutely revolting, thought Vanessa, as a dark shadow drew closer on the planked sidewalk.

"Help you, ma'am?"

It was Sheriff J. T. Sturgis again, tipping his hat, a sly smile on his face. I know what he wants, Vanessa thought, but he's not going to get it. "How does one cross the street without hiring a ferry?" she asked.

"You either walk, or git carried. Since you prob'ly don't want to git your pretty boots dirty, I'd be happy to do the honors."

She glanced away absent-mindedly, as he lifted her like a feather in his strong arms. Then he headed into the street, his tin badge about level with her left breast, while her rump rested in his muscular forearms. She decided that he wasn't bad-looking, if you appreciated the rugged sun-baked type (and she did).

"Have you changed your mind about dinner tonight?" he asked raffishly.

"No, thank you, but I can't help wondering — why would anybody want to become sheriff of Escondido?"

"I'm the meanest man in town, but I wouldn't be mean to you, Miss Fontaine. Besides, somebody's got to stand up fer the law, otherwise it's the end of the world."

An idealist with a gun, she thought, as they came to the sidewalk in front of the Last Chance Saloon. He let her slide down his hands to the sidewalk, and she felt his hands run up her body. It was so erotic she nearly swooned, but Vanessa had been trained from infancy to maintain outward control; otherwise men would hound her into the ground.

"Thank you," she said, adjusting her bonnet. "But I think hereafter that I'll be crossing the street myself."

"As long as there's men like me in the world, women like you'll never have to walk nowheres. Say, you weren't planning to go into that hellhole, were you?"

"As a matter of fact, I'd intended to speak with Miss Maggie O'Day."

"I'll introduce you to her, if you like. She's a friend of mine."

Cowboys, vaqueros, outlaws, and banditos stopped what they were doing to watch the tall beautiful blonde being escorted by the sheriff toward the front door of the Last Chance Saloon.

"Would I like to get some of *that*," murmured a thick masculine voice in the crowd.

Sheriff Sturgis pushed open the doors as if he owned the Last Chance Saloon, and every eye in the house turned toward the odd duo encroaching onto their midst. The sheriff's tin badge gleamed in the dimness of a large rectangular room as he led Vanessa among crowded tables. A bar was to the left, with a stage and small dance floor in back. Above the bar hung the usual lurid painting of a naked woman smiling at the men below.

"Who's the blonde?" somebody asked drunkenly.

"Tall drink of water, ain't she?"

Vanessa considered the interior unusually clean for a frontier saloon, with polished brass spittoons and no chicken or steak bones lying on the floor. The bartender wore a clean white shirt, and the waitresses appeared friendly, without too many teeth missing, all trying to comport themselves like ladies. Not a bad place after all, sniffed Vanessa, veteran of a career singing in saloons.

The sheriff led her down a corridor and knocked on the door. "Come in," said a gruff voice on the other side.

The sheriff stepped to the side as Vanessa entered the office in her usual grand manner. A heavyset middle-aged woman with dark blonde hair sat behind the desk, a glass of whiskey in one hand,

and a thick black cigar in the other.

"Who the hell're you?"

The sheriff made introductions. "I'm sure you ladies have got a lot to talk over," he said, "and there's a warrant I've got to serve, so I'll be a-wishin' the both of you goodday."

The sheriff retreated, leaving the two women to look each other up and down. "Have a seat," said Maggie finally. "What can I do fer you, Miss Fontaine?"

Vanessa sat on the plush green velvet chair in front of the desk and crossed her legs. "I'm looking for a man whom I understand was . . . friendly . . . with you. His name was Duane Braddock, and he was sheriff of this town."

There was silence in the office as Maggie puffed her cigar thoughtfully. "So yer the one," she said at last.

Vanessa was taken aback by her remark. "What do you mean?"

"He told me about the Charleston belle who became a saloon singer — am I right?"

"That's me," Vanessa admitted. "What else did he say?"

"You broke his heart, but he couldn't ferget you."

Thank God, thought Vanessa. "I made a

mistake," she confessed, "and I shouldn't've left him. He's got a right to hate me, but here I am searching for him anyway. I understand he's visiting Mexico."

"Last time I seen him, he was a-headin' fer the Rio Grande, and I reckon he's still south of border, a-waitin' the right time to come back. One of these nights he'll walk through the front door of this saloon, mark my words."

Vanessa looked over the plump, be-jeweled Maggie O'Day, and wondered if she was a rival. "Are you in love with him too?"

"Hell, all the women are in love with the Pecos Kid, but as far as I know, he didn't lay any one of us while he was here."

A tear came to Vanessa's eyes, but she wiped it away with the tip of a hand-kerchief. "I should never have given him up, but he'd only been out of the monastery a few weeks, and he was so poor. Then, when a certain army officer came along —"

"What happened to the army officer?" inquired Maggie.

"Killed in action against the Apache," replied Vanessa stiffly. "And now I want Duane back."

"Was he *that* good in bed?"

"I know what you're thinking," replied Miss Vanessa Fontaine. "I'm an older woman in love with a younger man, and I've lost my senses. Maybe you're right, but if you're a friend of Duane's, you'll help me find him. I happen to be quite wealthy now, and I intend to hire whatever lawyers, judges, and lawmen are necessary to quash all charges against him. I know him well, and don't believe that he's the cold-blooded killer everybody says."

"There's rage in that boy," replied Maggie, "and it really don't take much to tick him off. But you're right, it's usually some other galoot a-pushin' and a-shovin'. They're all jealous of him, because the gals are crazy about him, like you."

"And you?"

"Me?" Maggie laughed heartily. "I know that I look great and all that, but hell — let's face it — I'm old enough to be his mommy, and sometimes that's how I feel around him. He's a lost little boy, when he's not a-shootin' people, and he needs somebody to look out fer him. Did he ever tell you how his parents died?"

"His father was hung for a cattle rustler, and his mother disappeared under mysterious circumstances."

78

"T'weren't nawthin' mysterious. His mother had consumption most of her life, but his father weren't hung. No, he was gunned down by hired killers in the pay of Sam Archer of Edgeville, Texas. When Duane was in Escondido, some of Archer's hired guns tried to bushwhack 'im, but it din't turn out that way. Now old Sam Archer's in deep shit, because Duane Braddock is after him, and he ain't never a-gonna let go."

The room fell silent, as the two women measured each other relentlessly, like gunfighters ready to draw and fire. In Maggie's eyes, Vanessa was a lady who walked as if she had a broom stuck up her ass, while Vanessa considered Maggie a creature only slightly above the level of pig.

"I think I'll stay in Escondido for a while," said Vanessa, "and wait for Duane to arrive."

"He promised he'd come back here, and when a man like Duane Braddock promises something, you can build a house on it."

"How he must've changed," said Vanessa. "When I knew him, he appeared bewildered by life outside the monastery."

"He's not so bewildered anymore, and some of the old-timers say he's got the fastest hand they'd ever seen. I watched him draw on three men right outside my front door one night, and his hand moved so quick — you couldn't even see it, but he lived with Apaches for a spell, and he's part Apache his own damn self."

"Apaches?" asked Vanessa. "Sounds like he's been busy since I saw him last, but let me make a business proposition to you. I know all the good old tunes that your patrons love so well, and if you poster my name around town, I'll bring you business you never saw before."

Maggie had heard scraps of saloon information about Miss Vanessa Fontaine, the so-called Charleston Nightingale. "I'll give you a week's work, and if you increase my business, you can keep on as long as you like."

"I'm living at the hotel," said Vanessa, "and my accommodations are beyond human endurance. This looks like a large building, and I was wondering if you might have a few rooms that I could rent."

Maggie chortled. "This is a whorehouse, remember? If you live here, people will figger yer a whore like the rest of us."

"I don't care what people think," replied Vanessa. "I need to be comfortable, and I might as well open tomorrow night, to give you time to nail posters around town. It's called advance publicity, and it really pays off."

"I know yer game," Maggie said, leaning back and blowing smoke rings into the air. "Yer a-hopin' Duane Braddock'll see a poster, and come to see you."

The Charleston Nightingale rested her elbows on the desk, peered into Maggie's eyes, and said: "Exactly."

CHAPTER 4

A Moorish mansion surrounded by gardens and orchards loomed out of the night as Duane gazed through the stagecoach window. It was the largest building he'd ever seen, and he hadn't been aware that such places existed except in story books about kings and princes.

The hacienda was surrounded by barns and outbuildings, and lights shone in windows, while a crowd of well-dressed men and women gathered in the courtyard. In front stood a short, bald, portly gentleman with graying chinwhiskers, hat in hand.

"That's my father," said Doña Consuelo. "He is losing his health, because he worries so much about my mother."

Duane wanted to comfort her as she mourned the illness of her beloved mother.

What kind of beast am I to lust after this decent Catholic married woman? he asked himself.

"Is anything wrong?" she asked.

"My leg," he lied.

"You are a man of strange moods, but you will always be wonderful in my eyes, for my life literally belongs to you. I don't understand how you did it, because you were nearly killed."

"Luck," he replied, with a shrug. "And let's hope it continues."

The door opened, and the strong arms of a servant carried Doña Consuelo to the ground. Her father, Don Patricio de Vásquez, stepped forward to embrace her. "My dearest girl," he said. "I'm so happy to see you."

"How's mother?"

"Your visit will do her much good, I'm sure."

The courtyard became still as all eyes turned to the tall Americano stepping out of the stagecoach. He wore black clothes, with a black cowboy hat slanted low over his eyes, and a gun slung low, tied down, and ready for action.

Doña Consuelo explained: "This is a friend named Duane Braddock, and if it weren't for him, I'd probably be dead right now." She described the attack by banditos, the stagecoach out of control, and Duane appearing miraculously out of nowhere, diving onto the nigh leader, and bringing the team to a halt. "It was the most amazing feat of horsemanship I've ever seen," she declared, "although he'd been shot in the leg by banditos."

Don Patricio placed his arm around Duane's shoulder. "My daughter is my most precious possession, and you have given her back to me. Sir, I can never repay you enough, but please be my guest for as long as you like."

The gathering expected Duane to say something, and he felt deeply embarrassed. All he could mutter was, "It was my honor to be of service to your daughter, sir."

The crowd applauded, and Duane realized that he'd won them to his side. Evidently Doña Consuelo was much beloved by the peasants, and he could well understand why. "Folks have to help each other," he said, "no matter what country they're from."

"Well spoken," said Don Patricio, shaking Duane's hand. "Our two nations have taken up arms against each other in the past, but perhaps one day we can live in peace together, although it seems awfully unlikely, I admit."

Don Patricio barked orders to his servants. A middle-aged, well-barbered man in a white suit approached Duane and bowed. "Where is your luggage?"

Duane pointed to the saddlebags slung over his shoulder. "This is it."

"Please come with me, sir."

"What about my horse?"

"He will be well taken care of, sir."

"I'm awful fussy about my horse."

"This is a horse-breeding ranch, and we also raise fighting bulls for the arena. My name is Domingo, at your service."

Duane followed Domingo through a series of corridors with windows on both sides, as in the monastery in the clouds. They passed beneath arched doorways, while torches flamed along the walls, illuminating portraits of gentlemen, ladies, horses, and Mexican landscapes, plus paintings of religious themes. It was like a museum, and finally they came to a dark bedroom.

Domingo lit a candelabra on the dresser, illuminating a massive canopied bed. Thick violet curtains covered the windows, and there were upholstered chairs, dressers, a desk, and a three-way mirror. It was the closest Duane had come to luxurious living, and he stared like a country bumpkin.

"You would like a bath?" asked Domingo.

"Yes," replied Duane, "but I have no clean clothes."

"I'm sure that I can find whatever you need. Leave your dirty things out, and they'll be washed. A meal will be served within the hour, and someone will come for you. Or, if you prefer, you may wander wherever you like. We have a chapel and a library in back of the hacienda, you may be interested to know."

Domingo retired, and then two uniformed manservants carried an ornate porcelain tub into the room, followed by four additional liveried footmen with a barrel of hot water. They placed the tub near the open window, then poured water into it, the steam filling the air, and maids laid out fresh clothing on the bed. Meanwhile, other maids scooped up Duane's dirty clothes and mangled boots, while two more turned down his bed.

"Anything else, sir?" asked the maid, who wasn't much older than he.

My God, Duane thought, as he stared into her innocent eyes. "No, thank you, and if you don't mind, I'd like to be alone."

The maids withdrew silently, closing the door behind them. Duane drew his Colt, stood with his back against the drapes, and peered outside. The crowd had disappeared from the courtyard, and the stagecoach was on its way to the stable, followed by his unfaithful horse, Midnight.

Duane felt safe in the thick-walled hacienda. He wanted to drop to his knees, and thank *El Señor* for his good fortune, but didn't want the bathwater to get cold. It might be a good idea to get a shave, he figured. Duane meditated upon available funds as he sank into the hot bathwater. He had a few hundred dollars in American coins, which seemed a small fortune, but the wealth Duane now observed was beyond his wildest imagination.

He couldn't help reflecting on the strange twists and turns of a man's life. He'd been born on the dodge, raised in a monastery, worked as a cowboy, been a sheriff, and lived among the Apaches. Now he found himself in opulence, and all the money he'd earned in his life couldn't buy the bed.

The easy life has got to make people soft, he speculated. I'd rather sleep on the desert than that bed, because the desert will make you a warrior, while a bed will turn you into a lazy bummer, and you'll spend your life there with some Mexican maid.

The ceiling seemed to go on forever, like the roof of the church at the monastery in the clouds. He lay in the warm water, and let his thoughts float toward his hostess, Doña Consuelo de Rebozo. In many ways, he mused, she's even more beautiful than Miss Vanessa Fontaine.

He didn't like to think about Miss Vanessa Fontaine, but sometimes she popped into his mind at the damnedest times. The saloon singer had raised him to the empyrean heights of love, then ditched him for an Army officer, and Duane hadn't been right since. He'd become involved with other females subsequently, and nearly married a rancher's daughter once, but she got tired of the fugitive life, and returned to Daddy. Duane wanted to forget Miss Vanessa Fontaine, and was confident that he would as soon as he found another woman.

Whatever happens, I must never make a display of affection toward Doña Consuelo de Rebozo. This isn't a saloon prostitute that I'm talking about here, or even a woman of the world like Miss Vanessa Fontaine. Doña Señora de Rebozo is a real lady, and adultery is a mortal sin, especially when premeditated. If you ever lay even one hand on her, you'll go straight to hell, and the little red devils will put you into their hottest oven till the end of time.

A maid opened the door, and Doña Consuelo tiptoed into her mother's bedroom. Moonlight slanted through the open window, illuminating a frail figure in the middle of a large canopied bed. Tears filled Doña Consuelo's eyes, and she pulled a handkerchief out of her sleeve and daubed her eyes.

My poor dear mother, she thought, as she stood at the side of the bed. The matriarch had lost half her body weight, as the cancer ate her alive. She appeared ninety years old, with a faint slick of perspiration on her forehead. It was difficult to imagine that this dying old crone had been a vibrant middle-aged woman only a few years ago.

Doña Consuelo knelt at the side of the bed, clasped her hands together, and prayed: *Hail Mary, full of grace* . . . It didn't seem right that a religious woman like her mother should suffer, while killers and banditos lived forever. Where is the justice in the world? asked Doña Consuelo.

She knew the story of Job, and understood that ordinary people could never understand the mind of God. I'll be alone soon, she thought desperately. No one could ever appreciate me like my mother, who'd lived simply and righteously like a saint all her life.

"Oh, mother," whispered Doña Consuelo, "what will I do without you?"

The figure on the bed stirred. "Is that you, Consuelo?"

"How are you, mother?"

"Every day I grow weaker." It seemed an effort for the shriveled woman to speak.

"You'll be well in a few more months — I'm sure the doctors will help you. You must have faith, for Christ said that faith will move mountains."

"I'm too weak to have faith, daughter, but you must understand, after I'm gone, that if you want to be with me, just drop to your knees and pray. The way of the righteous leads to heaven, while the path of the evildoer leads to the flames of hell."

Doña Consuelo imagined a wall of flames arising from the wall, consuming all in its path. The young Catholic wife believed, deep in her heart, that hell was exactly like that, with sinners writhing and shrieking eternally over open fires.

The room was silent, except for her mother's shallow respirations. Doña Consuelo placed her warm hand on her mother's cool arm. Her heart filled with sorrow when she contemplated the suffering of the poor woman. It's better to die than linger this way, she considered. But she wanted to keep her mother as long as she could.

"How is your marriage going, my dear?" her mother asked in a whisper.

"I am very happy, mother."

"Are you . . . ?"

"Not yet, mother. Sometimes I think there is something wrong with me."

"Be patient, and don't forget: your husband is not a young man, either."

"But he's very young, mother. Vaqueros in their twenties can barely keep up with him."

Her mother smiled wisely, while Doña Consuelo wondered what the sick woman was trying to communicate. "He should be here soon," Doña Consuelo said. "He's most worried about you."

"I'm not worth everybody's trouble, and we all live at God's pleasure anyway."

Her faith is strong, Doña Consuelo realized. I hope, when my time comes, that I can be as strong as she. Doña Migdalia's eyes closed, as the exertion of speech exhausted her. Doña Consuelo stared at the outline of a skull lying on the pillow. From dust we come, and to dust we shall return, the daughter thought morosely. All our hopes and aspirations end in the grave, and there isn't anything we can do about it.

Doña Consuelo had never thought much about graves prior to the illness of her mother, but now Sister Death was haunting her home, about to take her mother away, and even she herself, Doña Consuelo of the barren womb, even she would end up in a dark dank hole in the ground, chewed upon by rats, nibbled by insects, and rotting like any other lump of dead meat.

Doña Consuelo nearly gagged at the mere contemplation of her own decaying bones. Yet it was no idle dream, but a true vision of her future. My days are numbered, and perhaps I can make better use of them. I should spend more time with the poor, and do charity work for the church, but nothing will ever take the place of my dear mother, who taught me all I know of life.

Tears streamed down Doña Consuelo's cheeks as she withdrew from the room.

She sat on a chair in the outside corridor and wept into her handkerchief, overwhelmed by the tragedy of life. Why do people have to die? she asked. What kind of strange horrid world do we live in, where our greatest achievements are made meaningless and even laughable by the plain ugly fact of death? Why do we have to live in the first place? What does it all mean?

Young Doña Consuelo was suffering her first crisis of faith, and it felt as if the world were disintegrating. She saw clearly the underlying truth that no one wanted to countenance: all living creatures were marching toward the grave, and when Sister Death struck, it was often quite painful, lingering, and dreadful for all concerned. Whether you live in the hacienda or the poorest shack in the village, we all end up in the same hole in the ground, and our lives are mere gusts of wind on the desert of time, deliberated Doña Consuelo.

She arose from the chair and wandered toward her room. One day this place will be dust too, and a new civilization will come on the heels of ours. All we can do is trust in God and follow His commandments. She noticed movement at the end of the corridor. Someone was wandering about, wearing black Mexican pants and a ruffled white shirt. "Who's there?"

"It's me," said Duane Braddock, "and I was looking for the library."

Doña Consuelo stared at him in the darkness, because she barely recognized him, clean-shaven in new clothes. He had a smooth, well-formed jawline, high cheekbones, and appeared extremely handsome. "It's at the back of the house. I'd be happy to show you where it is. You look so different without your beard."

"It's a chore to shave while you're living outdoors."

He reminded her of a painting of Jesus Christ by José de Ribera, the great baroque Spanish artist. Duane's Mexican suit appeared tailormade for his body; the pants were flared at the bottom, while his shirt had wide flowing sleeves. She noticed that he was carrying his pistol, as if he expected the U.S. Army to show up at any moment. There was something gentle and childlike about him, and he had soft eyes like a woman. My God, I wouldn't be surprised if he was the best-looking man I've ever seen in my life!

The thought delighted her, as she glanced at him sideways. Meanwhile, he stole a glimpse of her. Their eyes met for a brief shining instant, then both turned away.

"What were you doing in the corridor?" he asked.

"I've just left my mother's bedroom. She doesn't have much more time, and to tell you the truth, I don't know how I'll get along without her. Is your mother still alive?"

"No, she died about seventeen years ago."

"Do you miss her?"

"I hardly ever knew her, or my father either."

She wrinkled her pretty brow, as she came abreast of a door. "What a strange person you must be. Coincidentally, this is the entrance to our chapel. Would you mind if I stopped a moment and said a prayer for my mother?"

"I'll pray with you," replied Duane. "Lord knows, I've got a few things I worry about, too."

They entered the worship space, which was more capacious than churches in many small towns. It had stained glass windows, with a nave, transept and apse, and candles burning before statues of saints. They knelt in a pew, and Duane crossed himself reverently, clasped his hands together, and glanced at Doña Consuelo out the corner of his eye.

She was perched on her knees beside him, her hips and shoulders nearly touching his, her head bent forward, eyes closed in prayer. This is a fine, religious woman, he concluded, as he imagined her voluptuous nakedness, skin smooth as satin, and pink rosebuds on her breasts. Then he turned away, plagued by guilt and shame. The mere thought of her naked legs caused him to swoon, and he couldn't suppress a soft moan of desire.

"Are you all right?" she asked as she turned toward him abruptly. "Perhaps you'd better sit down."

"Yes, it's my leg again," he lied, as he slid onto the pew.

Still on her knees, she turned toward him. "We can rest awhile, but not too long. Dinner will be served shortly, and I'm starving to death." Then she bowed her head and returned to prayer.

She's at ease before the Lord, he realized, and that means she prays all the time. This is a woman who would never in her life entertain a foul thought, so why do I want to dive on top of her, wrestle her flat on the floor, and lie between her legs, grunting like a hog? There must be something wicked in my mind, to make me think this way. Oh Lord, please help me treat this woman with the utmost respect. I'm no angel, but even I draw the line somewhere.

This is the kind of woman whom I should marry when it's time to settle down, he lectured himself. I don't need more saloon singers, liars, or daddy's little girls. I just want someone with a sincere heart, who'll go that extra distance for me, instead of leaving when the going gets rough. This woman believes in deep things, not the wisdom of the moment. I'm probably falling in love with her, but what man in his right mind wouldn't?

He wanted to kneel in the pew with her, and touch his leg against hers. He could imagine no higher pleasure than unbuttoning the back of her dress. The skin on her throat appeared delicate, and he suspected it would burst and bleed profusely at the mere touch of a passionate tongue. He wanted to twist her into lascivious positions, and have his way with her like the old whoremaster he considered himself at the age of eighteen.

He caught his breath, appalled by such prurient thoughts. A lifetime of Catholic education has done nothing for me, but you don't go destroying other people's lives to satisfy your own animal lust. I may be a moral weakling and a physical coward, but I definitely have the strength to restrain myself in the presence of this woman, right?

Vanessa Fontaine sat before the mirror and carefully applied cosmetics to her face. She needed the audience to see her classically beautiful Anglo-Saxon features, because it was part of the illusion she sought to create, the better to capture the imagination of drunkards and fools.

Miss Vanessa Fontaine took her performing seriously, for she'd studied music as a child, and had viewed many great luminaries of the entertainment world at the theatres and music halls of Charleston. She'd even witnessed a performance by Jenny Lind during the celebrated Swedish Nightingale's 1851 American tour. That was the magic she was reaching for, as she applied rouge to her stark cheekbones. She loved applause and adulation, because it made her feel she couldn't be all bad.

There was a knock on the door, and Maggie O'Day appeared. "The saloon is packed to the rafters," she said happily. "Never seen nawthin' like it in all my days. The men're gittin' impatient, and I'm surprised nobody's shot a hole through the ceiling yet. You 'bout ready to go on?"

"You may introduce me," Vanessa said. "I'll be right out."

"Introduce you?" asked Maggie. "But . . . what should I say?"

"Whatever comes to mind. I'm sure you'll think of something, and now, if you'll excuse me, I'd like to be alone."

Too big fer her britches, Maggie thought, as she marched forthrightly through the network of corridors. But I guess she's worth it. Maggie could hear the grumbling and growling of men waiting for the opening night performance of Miss Vanessa Fontaine. She arrived in the main room of the saloon, and a sea of sombreros and cowboy hats spread before her, while a bullwhacker had shinnied halfway up a pole that held the roof. The Last Chance drew a substantial crowd on Saturday nights, but nothing like the horde before her. She'd followed Vanessa's instructions, and her employees had nailed posters all over the county. A surprisingly large number of men had heard of the Charleston Nightingale.

"Whar the hell is she?" asked a drunken cowboy standing nearby, a mug of beer in his hand.

"Be patient, gentlemen," replied Maggie. "She's on her way."

Maggie sauntered toward the stage, and if a drunkard wouldn't get out of her way, she unceremoniously pushed him to the side. She'd learned long ago that the only way to deal with outlaws was take no guff at all. The crowd shouted approval as she stepped onto the stage, and she blinked in the bright light of oil foot-lamps.

There was only one way to capture their attention, so she lifted the side of her skirt, yanked out her derringer, and held it up so all could see its ugly snubbed nose. The saloon became miraculously silent, for nothing sobers men quite like the sight of a woman with a gun in her hand.

Maggie smiled. "Howdy," she said in her whiskey- and tobacco-coarsened voice. "You damned sure ain't here to see me, but I want you to remember one thing. Our featured performer has travelled a long distance to entertain you fellers tonight, and I expect you to treat her like the lady that she is. So let's give a big Texas welcome to the woman you've all been waiting for, the world famous Charleston Nightingale, the one, the only — Miss Vanessa Fontaine!"

Applause rocked the saloon as a tall slim figure in an ankle-length mauve silk gown, trimmed with Malines lace and diamond puffs, appeared in the doorway. It was Miss Vanessa Fontaine herself, the Charleston Nightingale, on her way to the stage. She hoped that a certain green-eyed young man might be in the audience, having ridden countless miles to see her perform.

A path opened before her as she promenaded onward. Men pounded their hands, whistled, yelled, and jumped for joy. It was as though they were paying homage to a great goddess of their people, which in a sense Miss Vanessa Fontaine truly was. The bullwhacker who'd shinnied up the pole was grinning like a baboon.

Vanessa carried herself to center stage, unerringly found the best light, and took her first bow. Hats were thrown into the air, men hooted, and somebody fired his gun, installing the expected bullet hole through the ceiling. The report made Vanessa jump two inches in the air, and for a moment she'd thought that someone had assassinated her, but then she noticed the worshipful expressions in their eyes, and all she could do was bow again to the thunderous acclamation rolling across the dimly lit saloon.

She realized that they were slipping away

from her and becoming lost in an orgy of uncontrolled foolishness, so she raised her hand, smiled expectantly, and prepared to speak. Without a weapon in her hand, her simple gesture plunged the saloon into rare silence, except for the dripping of a bucket behind the bar.

"Gentlemen," she began, "I want to thank you for your gracious welcome, and I really don't believe you're a bunch of cattle rustlers, bank robbers, and hired killers, as some folks say. In any event, here we are together again, and I'd like to sing, with your permission, a few of the good old songs that we love so well. Although I'm standing up here in the lights, and you're down there in the audience, we've all lived together in a place you can't find on any maps, but that we'll always carry in our hearts. It was called Dixie, and I'd like you to sing along with me, if you'd be so kind."

There was no orchestra, conductor, or instruments. It was just Miss Vanessa Fontaine, one palm of her hand resting in the other, standing before them and opening her mouth to sing:

*"I wish I was in the land of cotton
Good times there are not forgotten*

Look away, look away, look away
Dixie land.
In Dixie land where I was born
in a shack on a frosty morning
look away, look away, look away
Dixie land . . ."

In truth, Miss Vanessa Fontaine had been born in the manor house, not a shack on a frosty morning, but many men in the audience had first seen the light of day in broken-down shacks, or sod houses, while others had been raised with silver spoons in their mouths. Her strong coloratura voice brought them back to those halcyon days, as she raised her arms dramatically, threw back her head, and belted out the chorus with all the musical gifts that God had given her:

"Then I wish I was in Dixie
Hooray! Hooray!
In Dixie land I'll make my stand
to live or die for Dixie!
Away, away,
Away down South in Dixie
Away, away,
away down South in Dixie!"

The saloon exploded with approval,

every voice singing loudly, for Dixie was no mere geographical location to Miss Vanessa Fontaine and the members of her audience. No, it was their spiritual landscape forged in flames, and they'd never forget languid summer afternoons, magnolia blossoms, mint juleps, and chivalry that the world had not seen for hundreds of years previously, and likely would never see again.

Miss Vanessa Fontaine bowed low, as if to acknowledge that men, not women, had charged batteries of cannon, been torn apart by rifle fire, and experienced the singular sensation of a cold, dirty bayonet in the guts.

Meanwhile, Maggie O'Day stood beside the bar, worrying that the volume of applause would blow out the very walls of her saloon. She'd employed the random fiddler or guitar plucker over the years, but never before had a performer like Miss Vanessa Fontaine stirred up such a tumult at the Last Chance Saloon. Coins showered upon the stage, and a gold twenty-dollar double eagle bounced off the Charleston Nightingale's nose as she arose and stood before them with her arms outstretched.

She's got that special something, no

doubt about it, thought Maggie O'Day. So this is the woman who captured young Duane Braddock's heart, threw it away, and now wishes she could get it back. Maggie wanted to hate Vanessa, but enjoyed a good show like the rest of her customers, who were drinking heavily and working themselves to fever pitch. She sells whisky, and that's all I care about, thought Maggie.

Meanwhile, at center stage, surrounded by a sea of gold and silver coins, Miss Vanessa Fontaine was preparing her next selection of the evening. Again she opened her mouth, and her voice filled the saloon:

"When the boys come home in triumph,
  brother
With the laurels they shall gain;
When we go to give them welcome, brother,
We shall look for you in vain.
We shall wait for your returning, brother
But you were set forever free;
For your comrades left you sleeping, brother,
Underneath a Southern tree."

Tears flowed copiously down the cheeks of gnarled old soldiers, as they recalled comrades they'd buried beneath southern trees. Vanessa's eyes weren't dry either, for her first love had fallen at Gettysburg, in the most immense cavalry engagement of the war. And her parents had died too, for the family plantation had lain unwittingly in the path of Sherman's cruel march to the sea. The song brought back beautiful and painful memories, as Vanessa and her audience became brothers and sisters of the great Lost Cause:

"You were the first on duty, brother
When 'to arms' your leader cried, —
You have left the ranks forever,
You have laid your arms aside.
From the awful scenes of battle, brother
You were set forever free;
When your comrades left you sleeping, brother
Underneath that Southern tree."

Pandemonium broke out in the Last Chance Saloon, as Vanessa curtsied demurely, spreading out her arms. More coins tinkled onto the stage, and she could tell by their number that she had been a success. She blew them kisses, for she truly loved them as they loved her, and she'd be nothing without their devotion and encouragement. She raised herself to her full height, and for the first time scanned their faces carefully, searching relentlessly for *him*. She prayed that she'd see his face in the adoring throngs, but failed to locate the black hat with silver concho hatband, and neither did she spot his eyes identical in color to hers, not to mention his Mona Lisa smirk. You could never figure out what was going on in that theological mind of his.

He's not here, she realized with dismay, as strange men proclaimed her name uproariously. But maybe he'll come tomorrow night, and all my dreams will come true.

Duane, Don Patricio, and Doña Consuelo were seated at one end of the long dining room table, as a servant placed a whole roast pig before them. The steaming beast was surrounded by silver bowls of yams, beans, rice, and tortillas. A guitarist strummed old Cadiz melodies in the corner, his sombrero covering his eyes.

Duane had never seen such extravagance, but he knew that peasants were gathered around nailed-together tables in the village below, or were seated on the floors of their humble adobe huts, with tortillas and beans if they were lucky, and a chunk of stray meat for flavoring, if God had been especially kind.

Supper was a sacrament to the poor, for food was so scarce, but in the hacienda it became a pageant with music by a skilled artist, the quantity excessive for three people, and everything seemed overdone, false, and effeminate to the Pecos Kid. He wasn't sure whether he liked it or not.

He gazed across the table at Doña Consuelo placing a forkful of pig into her shapely mouth. There was something compelling about the way she chewed; her jaws had a certain rhythmic motion, and he realized that he was staring at her.

Calmly, he returned his eyes to his plate. Her mother is dying upstairs, and I'm having carnal thoughts about Doña Consuelo. I studied for the priesthood, and here I am raping her in my mind. I must be one sick cowboy to be carrying on this way.

He turned toward Don Patricio, and wondered how a tubby old fellow with graying sidewhiskers and plump rosy cheeks could produce such a beautiful daughter. "I've never met anybody with more patience than your mother," said Don Patricio to Doña Consuelo. "How she tolerated me all these years is beyond comprehension."

"She loved you," the young wife replied,

"and she gave her life to all of us. I never appreciated her until now, and don't know how I'll get along without her."

Doña Consuelo went limp, and the fork fell from her hand. She seemed devastated by the impending death of her mother. A tear rolled down her cheek, and Duane wanted to comfort her, but instead took another slice of roast pig and another spoonful of beans.

"I've let her down on many occasions," confessed Don Patricio, "but it was easy to take advantage, because she was a saint. Some might have considered her weak, but only the truly strong can sacrifice for others. I will build a statue of her in the chapel, and dedicate it to the Virgin Mother."

"Perhaps if we tried another doctor," suggested Doña Consuelo in exasperation.

"We have the best doctors in attendance. Now it's in the hands of God, and all we can do is pray."

Duane observed the family interaction like a visitor from another realm. So this is what it's all about, the orphan boy cogitated. They relate their innermost thoughts, because they love each other. A family is a closeness that you just don't get in cantinas and saloons.

Footsteps rushed down the hall, and servants burst into the dining room. "Don Carlos has arrived!"

Doña Consuelo raised herself expectantly, then a tall silver-mustachioed nobleman strode into the dining room. Duane recognized him immediately — the caudillo he'd seen in Zumarraga.

Don Carlos advanced toward his wife, embraced her, and kissed her forehead. "I've heard that you were attacked by banditos, my dear."

"It's true," she replied. "The coachman and guard were killed, but this young man managed to stop the horses and save my life."

Don Carlos turned toward the clean-shaven young man sitting on the far side of the roast pig. "You look familiar. Have we met before?"

"A few nights ago in Zumarraga. My name is Duane Braddock."

Don Carlos smiled. "Of course — you wore a beard — I remember now."

Both men shook hands, and Doña Consuelo appeared flabbergasted. "You know each other?"

"In a manner of speaking," replied Don Carlos, who examined his guest with new interest. "I am greatly indebted to you for saving my wife, because she is the most valuable possession I have."

A servant piled food on Don Carlos's plate, as the caudillo looked at Doña Consuelo. "I will track the damned banditos down one of these days, and that will be the end of them." Then he glanced toward Duane. "Men usually run from trouble, but you rode into the middle of it to save someone you didn't even know. I can't help wondering — why?"

"So do I," replied Duane.

Doña Consuelo crossed herself reverently. "Señor Braddock was sent by God, and I would not be alive right now were it not for he."

Don Carlos nodded sagely. "Anything I have is yours, Señor Braddock. Just name it."

Your wife, thought Duane, but he didn't dare mouth the words. "I am honored to be of assistance, Don Carlos."

"Let's put our cards on the table," said the caudillo. "You are an American bandito, but that is no business of mine. You may stay at my hacienda for as long as you like, as my guest. If there's anything you require, you need only ask."

How about Doña Consuelo? Duane inquired silently. "You're very generous, sir, but I'll just need to rest my leg for a few days, and then be on my way."

"Come back later. My door is always open to you."

"According to the Bible, virtue is its own reward."

Don Carlos winked. "But a few extra pesos never hurt, eh?" Then he turned toward his wife. "And how is your mother, my dear?"

"Much worse, I am afraid. I wish we could find a *brujo* or somebody who could save her."

Duane watched Don Carlos converse with his wife, and felt jealous of the older man. Don Carlos sleeps with her every night, and places his hands on that cute little ass, while I'm always alone. What good does it do me to be well-educated, that I've got a fast hand, and see life with razor-sharp clarity? The only difference between me and the average filthy pig is I've got manners that I learned in the monastery in the clouds.

Miss Vanessa Fontaine sat before the mirror of her dressing room, her body soaked with perspiration. It was the same after every performance — she gave her audience everything, it was almost like making love. She wore a red silk robe embroidered with dragons, the gift of a former beau whose name she'd forgotten somewhere along her rocky road.

She felt disappointed that a certain familiar silver concho hatband hadn't appeared in the audience. She'd hoped Duane might've seen her poster nailed to a tree and come to claim her, but maybe he took one look and ran in the opposite direction, because she'd shattered his innocent seminarian's heart.

He truly loved me, she realized, and I was loco to leave him, but he hadn't a pot to piss in, while Lieutenant Dawes had been the son of a general, with a brilliant military career ahead of him, not to mention a substantial fortune left him by his grandfather. Vanessa had been low on funds, and decided to make a sensible decision for a change. She'd considered Duane a passing fancy, a pretty boy to play with for awhile, but never comprehended how much she'd fallen in love with him.

Why? she often wondered. Maybe it's the aura of danger that surrounds him, or his natural skills at making love. He wasn't afraid of any man, but his hair-trigger temper had been terrifying. She'd seen Duane shoot a dangerous gunfighter in a town called Titusville, the most shocking experience of her life on the frontier.

Duane Braddock, just out of the monastery, had faced off in the middle of the street against Saul Klevins, said to be the fastest hand in the county. The ex-acolyte had looked like a statue in the moonlight, the odds stacked against him, but he couldn't beg for his life. Klevins fired first, missed, and then Duane triggered, but his shot was true. He'd won the showdown, thanks to quick reflexes and the instruction of an old-time gunfighter named Clyde Butterfield. That's when a drunkard newspaper writer had dubbed Duane *The Pecos Kid*, thus launching his reputation, and now folks in West Texas mentioned him in the same breath as John Wesley Hardin and Jesse James.

One night, he will walk into this saloon, I can feel it in my bones, thought Vanessa. Because as good as it was for me, I know it was just as good for him, and he won't meet any others like me in his wanderings, just as I won't meet any other Duane Braddocks. All I have to do is wait, but when it comes to Duane Braddock, I've got nothing but time.

There was a knock on the door, and then Maggie O'Day walked into the dressing room, puffing a cigar. "What a show!" she exclaimed. "The first time I talked with you, I thought you were full of shit, but you really are a great singer — I've got to say it. Congratulations." Maggie slapped Vanessa on the back, and Vanessa nearly flew through her mirror. "By the way, the sheriff wants to talk with you."

"Tell him I'm busy."

"You don't understand, darlin'. You might need the sheriff on yer side if yer boy Duane Braddock ever shows up, because old J.T. will clap his ass in jail."

"Nobody'll ever put Duane Braddock in jail," replied Vanessa staunchly. "He'll die first."

"That's why you'd better talk with the sheriff. Let him know that Duane ain't as bad as his wanted poster would lead you to believe. I'd say that Duane'll be here in another four-five weeks, and that's why we gotta start a-workin' on the sheriff now. Otherwise we're a-gonna have a shoot-out in Escondido, and God only knows who'll get killed."

"I've talked to the sheriff already, and he's a hard case himself. What's your opinion of him?"

"Sturgis is mad as hell 'bout somethin', but I'll be damned if I know what it is."

"Send him in," replied Vanessa, as she patted her face gently with a moist dab of white cloth. "I'll try to talk sense to him."

The door closed, and Maggie's footsteps receded down the hall. Did Duane ever sleep with that old strumpet? Vanessa wondered. Presently there was a knock on the door, it opened, and a tin badge reflected in her mirror.

Sheriff J. T. Sturgis strode into the tiny dressing room, hat in hand. "Sorry to bother you, ma'am, but I wanted to tell you how much I enjoyed yer performance. I was in the war myself, and we used to sing them same songs around the campfires. You sure brought it all back."

"What unit were you with?" she inquired.

"I served under General George Edward Pickett."

He didn't have to say more, because all Southerners revered General Pickett, who'd led the most famous charge of the war. "I was never a soldier," admitted Vanessa, "but the war came to me when we lived in South Carolina, and my home was burned by the damned Yankees. Confederate soldiers are all heroes as far as I'm concerned, and nothing's too good for them."

Sheriff Sturgis balled his fist and bared his teeth. "The Yankees beat us, Miss

Fontaine, but not because they were better men. They had more of everything and it weren't a fair fight, but we couldn't let them boss us around."

"Certainly not," replied Vanessa, and she wasn't acting one bit. "People say forgive and forget, and maybe they're right, but I'm afraid I can't forgive General Sherman for what he did to South Carolina, and I'll never forget Dixie land."

"Neither will I," replied ex-Corporal Sturgis. "And I want to tell you somethin' else. I think yer just about the most beautiful woman I've ever seen, and I was a-wonderin' why you won't let me buy you supper sometime."

She smiled politely. "If you want to talk, pull up a chair and take a load off your feet. I have an hour till my next performance, and besides, you should know that I'm already spoken for."

He frowned. "Braddock? But he's on the dodge, and I'm right hyar. Hell, I'll marry you tomorrow mornin' if you want. I'll even give you a baby. And you could do a lot worse, believe me."

Vanessa wasn't surprised by his declaration, because men had been making similar admissions practically from the time she could walk, and it was a natural part of her

117

environment, like the sun and rain. "I'm touched by your proposition," she replied, "and you're certainly a fine-looking gentleman. Perhaps, in other circumstances, who could say what might happen? But now I'm waiting for Mister Braddock to return. If you want to be my friend, why don't you do me a favor? When he arrives, I hope you won't start trouble. My intention is to hire as many lawyers as necessary to clear his name, because he really hasn't committed any crimes as far as I know."

"Tell that to the trooper who survived the Devil's Creek Massacre."

"How can you condemn a man on the basis of one eyewitness who was half dead?"

"They say that when you love somebody, you can't think straight about him," Sturgis reminded her. "If Duane Braddock threw a baby off the roof of this building, and the whole town saw it, you'd say it was a mistake, and besides, the baby probably deserved it."

"You've never met Duane Braddock, and all you know is hearsay. Why not let the legal process do its job?"

The sheriff grinned. "I *am* the legal process, and I've got a warrant for Duane Braddock's arrest, dead or alive. Nobody'll take this badge seriously if I let a known killer walk around scot free. I'm sorry, ma'am, but that's one thing I can't do."

She raised a skeptical eyebrow. "A few minutes ago, you said that you'd marry me, but you won't do that little favor?"

"Ma'am, you're askin' me to violate my oath of office."

"What if I were to give you a hundred dollars to look the other way?"

"I'm not the best sheriff money can buy," he said bitterly.

"I didn't mean to insult you, but I'm absolutely convinced of Duane's innocence. I've personally witnessed one of his alleged crimes, and he was only defending himself."

"I'll bet he was only defending himself against that Army pay wagon too?"

Vanessa realized it was hopeless, but had to make one last try. "There's nothing I can do to change your mind?" she asked plaintively.

He looked her up and down, then his face grew red. It appeared that he wanted to say something, but refused to let it out.

"I'm sorry," she told him, "but that I can't do."

After supper, Duane wandered into the

small village alongside the hacienda. He heard guitars, and a man sang plaintively not far away. Duane wondered if there was a cantina where he could have a drink and think things over. Something told him to hop on Midnight and ride the hell out of there first thing in the morning, before he made a fool of himself with Doña Consuelo. Maybe I should go with a prostitute and get this out of my system.

He noticed lamps shining inside a squat adobe building. The door opened, and two vaqueros appeared, wearing big sombreros on the backs of their heads. "Is this the cantina?" asked Duane.

"Si, señor."

Duane entered the small, dark enclosure, stood in the shadows, and reconnoitered the territory. A painting of the Madonna and child was nailed to the wall, the bar wasn't crowded, and Duane leaned his elbow upon it. "Mescal."

The bartender was a dark-skinned Mexican with strong Indian features. "So you are the Americano who saved Doña Consuelo's life. On the house, señor."

All eyes turned toward Duane, and once again he was center of attention, the role he detested most. But he couldn't crawl underneath the cuspidor, so he raised his glass in the air, and said: "To Doña Consuelo."

No one could refuse a toast to the young lady of the hacienda, and all men raised their glasses to their lips. Duane advanced toward a table against the left wall, sat, and swallowed mescal. The other customers returned to their cards, newspapers, or conversations, as the Americano faded into the woodwork.

Duane toyed with the notion of seducing Doña Consuelo de Rebozo. What if I met her in one of those dark corridors when I return to the hacienda later tonight? Suppose I bent over and kissed her throat. I wonder if she'd call the guards, or maybe she wants me as much as I want her?

He realized that he was thinking disrespectfully about her again. Maybe I should ride away immediately, before I do something that I regret. Don't look for trouble, my friend. You've got more than you can handle as it is.

Duane scanned the cantina relentlessly, alert for trouble. He never knew when a bounty hunter or Pinkerton man would show up with a warrant for the arrest of the Pecos Kid. But the cantina was full of dark-skinned Mexicans like the bartender, and they reminded Duane of the Apaches.

Will they be insulted if I ride away first thing in the morning, and not even say good-bye?

He remembered Doña Consuelo kneeling beside him, saying her evening prayers. I almost jumped on top of her, and I wonder what silky things she wears underneath those long dresses of hers. I'll bet she goes wild when she gets naked, because it's always the nice girls who are the most wanton in bed.

I've got to stop thinking about her, he admonished himself, as he raised the mescal to his lips. And this is the best way to forget. He drained the glass, coughed a few times, then carried the glass to the bar and got a refill.

He felt lightheaded in the dark gloomy cantina, but it didn't prevent him from checking the position of men's hands. Occasionally he noticed somebody glancing at him, but the Mexicans didn't appear hostile. Fortunately or unfortunately, depending upon one's point of view, no prostitutes were in the small cantina. I'm in love with another man's wife — just what I need, he thought disgustedly. Vanessa Fontaine said she loved me, and she ran off with that damned army idiot. Phyllis Thornton said she loved me, and she went home to daddy. Love is a disease, and it looks like I've caught another dose. Doña Consuelo is a married woman, and I've got to stay away from her. *Whom God hath joined together, let no man put asunder.*

On the other side of the saloon, a Mexican drifter named Miguel Torres was passed out cold at a table. He'd been drinking mescal for the past three hours, his pocket was empty, and he was oblivious to the world. He snored with his face in a puddle of spilled liquor, cigarette ashes, and an old deck of cards.

Vagabonds, vaqueros, and banditos passed Miguel's table, but one happened to bump him by mistake. Miguel opened his eyes, and at first didn't remember who or where he was. Drunk again, he thought, as he pushed himself upright at the table.

It was late, he wanted to go to sleep, and planned to spend the night on the open desert, with one eye open for spiders, lizards, wildcats, and Apaches. His bleary eyes searched for an old companero to buy him one last glass of mescal, but then he noticed a gringo sitting alone against the left wall, peering into his glass. My God! thought Miguel. It can't be! He staggered to the bar, an expression of horror on his face.

"What is wrong with you?" asked the man in the apron. "You look as if you have seen a ghost."

"It is worse than that," whispered Miguel, as he pointed his thumb over his shoulder. "Do you know who is sitting over there — the gringo with the long sideburns down to here?"

The bartender squinted. "That is the man who saved the life of Doña Consuelo."

"Maybe so," said Miguel knowingly, "but he is also one of the most wanted men in *Tejas*."

The bartender appeared surprised. "You have been drinking too much mescal, my friend."

"No — that is Duane Braddock, known as the Pecos Kid, and he has killed nearly twenty men, and maybe more, no one can say for sure. I saw him shoot three with my own eyes in Escondido about two months ago. He is very *peligroso*."

The bartender smiled indulgently. "But he is so young, and has the face of a baby. Are you sure he is the same gringo?"

"I would bet my life on it," said Miguel, as a crowd of curious vaqueros formed around him. "Desperadoes tried to ambush him on the main street, and he moved so fast — I never saw anything like it in my life. It was as though he was a *brujo,* and nobody could kill him."

A big, brawny vaquero sitting at the bar scowled in disbelief. "That gringo over there? You cannot be serious, companero. He is just a boy."

"He may look like a boy, but he does not kill like a boy. The whole Americano Army is looking for him, he is so bad. Sitting over there, *amigos,* is one of the worst killers who has ever been born."

Duane became aware that vaqueros at the bar were looking at him, and guessed that he'd been recognized. It seemed that no matter where he went, there was always somebody who'd heard of the Pecos Kid. He didn't like the attention, so he tossed down the remainder of his mescal, adjusted his black cowboy hat, and strolled out of the small dark cantina.

A vaquero lay on the sidewalk, and Duane kneeled to see if he was alive. "Are you all right?" Duane asked, rolling the vaquero onto his back.

"Where am I?"

"If you're not careful, one of these

drunkards is liable to step on you. Here —
let me drag you into that alley." Duane
helpfully took the vaquero by the armpits
and tugged him into the alley next to the
cantina, where another drunkard snored
loudly.

"Is there a *casa de putas* in this town?"
asked Duane, as he lowered the drunkard's
head to the ground.

"You will have to go to the next town."

Women are always the problem, figured
Duane, as he left the alley. They drive us to
drink with their damned shenanigans, and
then we start shooting each other over
them. Meanwhile, they act like innocent
angels, with their every movement and
article of dress calculated to drive us
totally out of our birds.

He kicked an empty can that lay in his
path, and it went sailing into the night,
reflecting the light of the moon. But it's
not women's fault entirely, he mentalized,
because they're not even aware of the
things they do. You can't blame them
because they're pretty and cute, and they
shake their fannies in that certain provoca-
tive way. It's how God made us, and we
just follow our instincts, not much different from bulls chasing cows on the
range, or eagles screwing high in the sky.

It's the law of nature, and even Jesus admitted that it's not a perfect world.

He came to the outer grounds of the hacienda, and decided to ride away first thing in the morning, without saying good-bye to his hosts and hostesses. But he wanted to see Doña Consuelo once more. I know I don't have a prayer with her, and such a woman wouldn't look twice at a dumb kid like me. I'd rather get hit in the guts with an Apache lance than feel this way about a woman.

He stopped next to a juniper tree, weak in the knees, unable to accept what was happening to him. I was in love with Vanessa, then Phyllis, and now I'm going through the whole mess again, except I'm never going to get my hands on her.

He recalled that he'd reached the same conclusion about Vanessa and Phyllis, but had ended up in bed with both of them, much to the surprise of all concerned. But neither were married, while Doña Consuelo was a married Catholic woman. She would never in a million years take off her pantaloons for a man like me, but maybe I'll hang around for a few more days, because you never know.

An armed vaquero opened the front door, and Duane made his way down the long torchlit corridor, heading for his bedroom. He realized that *she* was sleeping somewhere in that very building, probably wearing a fancy satin nightgown. He wished he could join her, and slowly, gently, raise the hem. The mere thought made him pant with desire, and he felt as if his head would explode.

She's probably screwing her husband right now, he figured. You can see how much she loves him, the way she hangs on his every word. Besides, marriage is one of the sacraments, and you mess with the sacraments, you're *really* in trouble. Just keep your hands to yourself, always be a gentleman, and never, under any circumstances, let yourself be alone with her.

On the other side of the courtyard, in one of those darkened rooms, Doña Consuelo lay in bed, waiting for her husband to join her. She could hear him fussing in the next room, removing his corset, while she wore a gown of spotless white silk trimmed with blue embroidery.

Doña Consuelo was despondent over her mother's steady decline, and feared that the old lady would die at any moment. The dutiful daughter felt alone, lost, and fearful of the future. Sometimes it seemed that her life was a sham, and she could find no good reason why she resided in the hacienda, while others slept in mud huts.

Her husband entered the room, and she breathed a sigh of relief. He would comfort her with love, and banish unworthy considerations. Perhaps they could bring new life into the world, to replace the spirit of death that hovered over the hacienda.

"Darling," she said, as she reached for him.

"I'm tired," he wheezed, as he pushed her away gently. "It's been a long day."

She didn't say a word, and felt embarrassed by lust for her husband. He generously hugged her, kissed the tip of her nose, then rolled away and closed his eyes. Doña Consuelo ground her teeth together in the darkness, because she was twenty-one years old, and there was a certain something she needed. She knew exactly what it was, felt mortified, and squiggled to the far side of the bed.

She felt strangely bereft, guilty, and confused. Perhaps I'm too hot-blooded for my own good, she deliberated. Maybe there's something wrong with my mind, since I want it so often. After all, my husband has a difficult life, he works from sunup till he goes to bed, and I mustn't make additional demands. Once or twice a month should be enough for any normal woman.

She rolled over and viewed the finely chiseled profile of her husband in the moonlight. He had a head of hair like a lion, and even in repose was a sight to behold. He looked like a monument, and greatness radiated from his every pore. She moved closer, to get a better look at his regal countenance. Moonlight revealed pouches beneath his eyes, deep lines around his mouth, and that bag of loose flesh under his chin. He was becoming ancient before her very eyes, but she'd always been attracted to older men, because they seemed more confident.

Doña Consuelo was tempted to cuddle with her husband, but didn't want to disturb his sleep. She remembered their glorious wedding night, when he'd initiated her into the rites of love, and could feel his body heat radiating across the mattress. She wondered what would happen if she crawled on top of him, or performed some other disgraceful act, but couldn't bring herself to make the advance. Decent women don't beg for fornication like squealing cats in heat, she reproached herself.

She rolled away and tried to calm down,

but hadn't felt so rambunctious since she couldn't remember when. Actually, the uneasy feelings had begun long before her husband had arrived for supper. In the chapel, when she'd been on her knees beside the young gringo, she'd experienced certain unmentionable sensations. He'd appeared greatly agitated too, and she'd feared that he'd attack her, throw her onto the floor, and ravish her shamelessly.

Now that she thought about it, he was the strangest young man she'd ever known, not that she'd met many. Duane Braddock moved with languid grace, but lacked the supreme dignity of her husband. The young gringo was strong and sinewy, tanned like an Indian, with flashing eyes and a self-conscious smile. Doña Consuelo experienced certain feelings that she refused to think about, so she wiped them out of her mind, rolled over, and tried to sleep.

Her husband snored softly, while she insisted on thinking disreputable thoughts about a certain young man. What if he came up behind me right now, hugged me tightly, and kissed the back of my neck? Her body felt curiously alive, while her mind was plagued by Catholic guilt. Christ said if we commit sins in our mind, it's as bad as committing them in reality, she sermonized to herself, as she reached for the rosary that hung on the bedpost for just such an emergency. She took it in her hands, and began to rattle the beads in the darkness, as her husband slept beside her like a beached whale. "Hail Mary, full of grace . . ." she whispered to the night, as she struggled to overcome her deepest needs.

Sheriff J. T. Sturgis returned to his office, troubled by his conversation with Miss Vanessa Fontaine. Despite her sweet voice and ladylike manners, her eyes hadn't flickered once with romantic curiosity, and she hadn't flirted the way a woman does when she wants a man. He realized with dismay that there was nothing he could say or do to make her love him.

He looked in the mirror, but his face didn't seem so hideous. At least he was honest, and didn't view murder as an inconvenience to be overcome with lawyers. Sheriff J. T. Sturgis had strong feelings about justice, and believed that God had talked to him in the midst of Pickett's famous charge.

In times of stress and confusion, he often relived those deafening minutes. His right hand trembled as he conjured the continual hail of massed Yankee rifleshots, cannons hurling razor-edged metal at the gray-uniformed warriors charging into the very maw of hell. Corporal J. T. Sturgis had thought he'd die at any moment, and even in the "Bloody Angle", where heaps of dead soldiers lay everywhere, he had still maintained his headlong charge.

It was slashing, slicing, and bashing eyeball to eyeball with Yankees from Maine and Vermont. He himself had been covered with blood and gore, and had been bellowing like a wild bull, until finally, barely perceptibly, he became aware that the center division was giving ground before the furious enemy onslaught.

Sturgis's eyes filled with tears as he recalled close friends ripped apart all around him, as bullets had whistled past his ears. He'd run for his life, and somehow, amid unspeakable carnage, he'd made it back to Confederate lines without one scratch, a miracle whose significance he still was trying to plumb. As near as he could figure it, God had spared his life for a purpose, and J. T. Sturgis had to devote himself to holy work for the rest of his life.

After Appomattox, he'd wondered how to fulfill his vow to the Almighty. Yankee injustice had continued during Reconstruction, in his opinion, so he'd joined the Klan, and when the Federal government clamped down, he'd drifted west, finally becoming a lawman. But his covenant with God had remained the same, to fight injustice in a violent and dangerous world.

He saw himself as a knight of the round table, not an ordinary cowboy or hardware salesman. He'd hoped that Miss Vanessa Fontaine would become his queen, except she believed she was above the law, and actually had tried to bribe him with a few gold coins.

Sturgis propelled himself from his chair, opened a drawer of his file cabinet, and riffled through documents, letters, and wanted posters. Finally he found the file on Duane Braddock, sat in the chair, and proceeded to read. The documents consisted mainly of communications from the Federal Marshal in San Antonio, and Fourth Cavalry headquarters at Fort Richardson. They listed Duane Braddock's many alleged crimes, and according to the latest count, the so-called Pecos Kid had killed approximately twenty-five men in Texas, and God only knew the tally from Mexico. According to a Fourth Cavalry directive:

Duane Braddock is extremely skilled in the use of arms, and no officer should attempt to apprehend him alone. Braddock never hesitates to shoot, and has demonstrated high accuracy in the past. It's best to catch him unawares, and if you draw your gun in his vicinity, be prepared to use it.

Sounds like a real bad egg, thought Sturgis. He raised his Remington, flipped the cylinder, and spun it with the palm of his hand. Then he snapped it into position and took aim at the front door. Come on, Mister Pecos Kid, or whoever else you think you are. If I could survive Pickett's Charge, I damn sure can handle one crazy trigger-happy kid like you.

CHAPTER 5

Don Carlos sucked in his gut as a man-servant laced up the girdle. The gap seemed to widen every day, and Don Carlos was chagrined to notice yet again that he was becoming an old man with a pot belly, his worst nightmare come true.

He looked at himself in the mirror, and loose flesh hung where straps of muscle had once bound his bones. He seemed constantly tired, but pushed himself hard, because he couldn't let it show. Men won't follow if you lack vitality, and nobody will respect you, he believed.

He heard a splash in the next room, where his wife was bathing behind closed doors, attended by her maids. Don Carlos imagined streams of foaming liquid flowing across her smooth pink skin. It was immensely flattering to be married to a young woman, but Don Carlos was unable to conceal advancing age, and sometimes feared that people were laughing up their sleeves at him.

Some days he felt better than any young man in the world, but other times his feet dragged and he found himself over the hill. Doña Consuelo should have a man her own age, he admitted to himself, but instead she's stuck with me. On the other hand, our marriage is based on deeply shared beliefs, not cheap physical attraction. We are soul mates, despite the difference in our ages, and she is the jewel of my heart.

There was a knock on the door, and a moment later a manservant appeared. "Don Patricio would like to speak with you, sir. He says it is very important."

Don Carlos buttoned the shirt over his girdle, as his face turned purple due to constricted blood vessels. "Send him in."

The manservant departed, then Don Patricio advanced into the room. "I have learned something interesting about our house guest," he said confidentially. "It seems that he went to the cantina for a drink last night, and a drifter recognized him. You may be interested to know that

Duane Braddock is one of the most notorious *pistoleros* in America, and even the Americano Army is looking for him."

Don Carlos wasn't especially surprised by the news, because he'd never forgotten the knife fight in Zumarraga. "But he saved Doña Consuelo's life, and has been on his best behavior here."

"You're right — we can't ask him to leave. I'll have my servants keep their eyes open for missing articles."

"I think we should give him the benefit of the doubt, and besides, perhaps the drifter had drunk too much mescal, and confused Braddock with somebody else."

Don Patricio departed as a servant helped Don Carlos with his black leather riding jacket. Don Carlos looked at himself in the mirror, and was pleased to note his flattened stomach. What a sly one Duane Braddock turned out to be, thought Don Carlos. But I don't care who he's killed, as long as he behaves himself around here.

Don Carlos dismissed his servants, then entered the room where Doña Consuelo was enjoying her morning bath. She lay resplendent in her porcelain tub, a towel wrapped around her hair, as maids rubbed her skin with soft soapy wash cloths. "I'd like to speak with you alone," he said.

She glanced at him curiously, pink and sweet-smelling in the tub. "Leave us," she ordered the maids.

They departed, and she looked at her proud caudillo, his steely mustache carefully twirled, jaw like a block of granite, stomach repressed by 19th-century girdle technology. He opened his mouth and said casually, "I don't want to frighten you, but it appears that Duane Braddock is wanted for a series of murders in *Tejas*. Last night, he was recognized in a cantina, but your father and I have decided that we shouldn't say anything, out of regard for his bravery. Hopefully, he'll be gone in a few days, but be careful around him, understand? Perhaps you should never be alone with him, to be on the safe side."

Doña Consuelo was aghast. "He certainly didn't seem like a killer to me, and happens to be a very religious young man. We've even prayed together."

Don Carlos smiled indulgently. "You're an innocent child, and don't understand that some people can act decently while plotting the most horrendous crimes. No, we can't take chances with this fellow."

"But we sat in the coach and held many conversations. He's very well-educated, and in fact was raised in a monastery."

Don Carlos was surprised by this item of news. "How do you know he's not lying?"

"He knows theology very well, and even studied St. Thomas Aquinas."

Her husband winked condescendingly. "I don't think it would take much to fool you, my dear. You're my precious flower, whom I protect from the ugliness of life, but now a dangerous gringo is living in our midst. Please be cautious, *mariposita*. Don't ever be alone with him."

"I'll stay in my rooms until he's gone, except for meals. And speaking of meals, it's time for breakfast. Please leave me alone, so that I can get dressed."

She ordered him about like a servant, which he found amusing. It gives her a sense of power that she actually doesn't have, he thought wryly, as he departed the room.

Doña Consuelo called back her maids, who rinsed, dried, and helped dress her in front of the mirror. The young wife looked at herself from all the angles as her maids brushed her long wavy hair. She brought her face close to the mirror, and her critical eyes spotted countless crevices. I'm getting wrinkled, old, fat, and ugly, she said to herself. Life is passing me by. I never accomplish anything, and

I'm not having any fun.

She put on a dark blue skirt and a white ruffled blouse that buttoned high up on her neck. Then she climbed to the top floor of the hacienda, where her mother's bedchamber was located. Doña Consuelo entered the dark room, and her mother lay still on the bed, fast asleep, an expression of peace on her face. Doña Consuelo kneeled beside her, and reached for her hand. "Oh, Mother, you're the only one who ever understood me, and you always knew what to do."

Doña Migdalia's fingers felt limp and cold, and Doña Consuelo experienced a bolt of fear. The young noblewoman leaned over the body, but her mother wasn't breathing, her lips slightly parted, her eyes closed. "Mother?" asked Doña Consuelo, taking a step back from the bed. "My God!" She felt frantically for a pulse, but there was nothing. A mirror lay on the nighttable, and Doña Consuelo held it in front of the old lady's nose. It didn't fog. "No!" screamed Doña Consuelo at the top of her lungs. "No!"

Maids and footmen rushed into the bedroom, as Doña Consuelo dropped to her knees beside the bed, and covered her face with her hands. "My mother's dead," she said softly, "and God help us all." She fainted, and only the quick hands of a servant prevented her head from crashing into the floor.

Duane reached for his Colt when he heard Consuelo's scream. "What's wrong?" he asked a guard in the corridor.

"Nothing to worry about, señor."

Duane resumed dressing in his bedroom. She probably saw a mouse, he figured. It's the way women exercise their lungs. He buttoned his shirt, as he recalled shouting matches with Miss Vanessa Fontaine, the woman who'd ruined his life, or so he thought.

It bothered him to recall her slinky sinuous ways, yet he couldn't help comparing her to Doña Consuelo de Rebozo. But it was like judging between a diamond and a pearl. The power of women terrified him, and often he recalled the wisdom of St. Paul, Apostle to the Gentiles:

It is better to marry than burn.

He parted his long black hair on the side, and was dressed like an American cowboy again instead of a Mexican nobleman. He gazed at himself in the mirror and wondered whether he was handsome. Some women had praised him, others treated him like a toad, and he had no idea what he represented to them. The former monk struggled to figure out life, but the more he investigated, the more incomprehensible it became.

He made his way down tapestried corridors, and found himself in the dining room. Three places were set, and a group of servants stood in the corner, talking in low tones. Duane sat, waiting patiently for breakfast to be served.

Then Don Carlos entered from the far side of the room, a stern expression on his face. He walked to the chair opposite Duane, seated himself, and said: "Doña Consuelo's mother has died during the night."

Duane remembered Doña Consuelo's scream, and felt saddened by her grief. "I'm sorry to hear that, sir. Please convey my condolences to your wife."

Don Carlos studied the notorious American outlaw seated before him. "Is your mother alive?" he asked, out of curiosity.

"No."

"Doña Consuelo was very attached to hers. This is a terrible blow to her."

"At least she still has you and her father,

so she's not completely alone."

Like you? wondered Don Carlos. The nobleman didn't know whether he liked Duane, or felt sorry for him. "The household is in turmoil, as I'm sure you can understand."

"Don't worry about me," replied Duane. "I'll eat in the bunkhouse with the vaqueros."

"That won't be necessary, but the level of service might not be as formerly. If it hadn't been for you, we'd have had two funerals in this home, and you can't imagine how much Don Patricio and I love young Doña Consuelo."

Oh, yes I can, thought Duane.

Doña Consuelo lay clothed but shoeless atop her bed, and felt terrible emptiness. "How can I live without my sainted mother?" she whispered, as she reached for the handkerchief folded neatly beside her.

She dabbed her eyes, sniffled, and then went slack, overwhelmed by the enormity of death. One moment we're here, next moment we're gone. She wondered where her mother was at that moment.

The climate necessitated a fast funeral, which would take place that day. Doña Consuelo didn't know how she could manage, but her mother had always maintained her poise, no matter what catastrophe had befallen the hacienda. Once upon a time, my mother was as young as I, reflected Doña Consuelo. The cycle of life goes on, except I'm a barren woman, and no child will mourn for me.

The death of her mother had shattered conventional avenues of thought, and her mind burst with notions that she normally suppressed. Doña Consuelo felt useless, hopeless, and damned to an unfulfilled future. A great yawning chasm opened before her, and she became terrified. I'm alone, with no one to talk with except my husband, but he thinks I'm a silly child, and he's probably right.

She reproached herself for worrying about herself more than others. I must go to my father and comfort him, except who'll comfort me? She rolled out of bed, took a few unsteady steps, and looked out the window. A hammering came to her ears as the carpenter nailed together a coffin in one of the outbuildings, while behind the chapel someone was digging a grave. Doña Consuelo didn't know whether to scream, cry softly, or run a hundred miles. Death was terrifying to the coddled and sheltered young woman.

She looked at her tear-stained face in the mirror, her hair sticking weirdly in all directions. Maybe I should talk to the priest, but he'll just pat my head as if I were a dog, and tell me to have faith in God.

She wondered why she was so alone, without sisters, brothers, or friends. Perhaps I should renounce everything and go to a nunnery, because I have nothing to live for. I'm not a good wife to my husband, because I can't have a child.

She thought of hurling herself out the window, but what good would that accomplish? Perhaps I'd better go to the chapel, get down on my knees, and pray. She laced on her shoes, not bothering to call a maid. Then she put a dark shawl over her shoulders and made her way unsteadily toward the chapel.

Tears streamed down her cheeks, which she daubed with a handkerchief. Her vision blurred, and her legs felt like long enchiladas stuffed with melted cheese. I can't go on, but I must, she told herself. My mother would be ashamed of me if she could see me right now.

She paused near a bend in the corridor to catch her breath. Somehow I've got to be strong, she encouraged herself. No man wants a crybaby for a wife.

She tried to stiffen her spine as voices came to her from around the corner. Maids were having a private whispered conversation only a few feet away, and Doña Consuelo didn't know whether to interrupt or make believe they weren't there.

"I think it is disgusting," said one of the maids, and Doña Consuelo recognized her voice as Teresa's.

"What a hypocrite Don Patricio is," agreed another maid, named Florianna. "He is crying like a baby, but meanwhile he has kept that woman in town all these years."

"Crocodile tears," replied Teresa.

The voices became faint as the maids walked away. Doña Consuelo stood with her shoulder leaning against the wall, and her mouth hanging open. My father has kept a woman in town? I don't believe a word of it. Doña Consuelo teetered toward the chapel, telling herself that she really hadn't heard the previous conversation, although she knew, deep in her heart, that she had.

The stable was immense, filled with muscled steeds in large stalls, while a crew of vaqueros was sweeping, shoveling, and caring for the expensive animals. Duane made his way down the center aisle, admiring the Vásquez and Rebozo personal stock. These horses probably live better than most people, decided the Pecos Kid.

He spotted Midnight on the left aisle. "How's it going, boy?" he asked, as he stood before the trough into which Midnight dipped his snout.

Midnight raised his head sullenly. So it's you.

"I've been worried about you," Duane said. "Are they taking good care of you?"

If you're so worried, how come this is the first time you've come around?

Duane felt uneasy as Midnight's bulbous eyes drilled into him. "I've been awful busy," he explained, "and let's not forget that I've been shot in the leg."

You don't look so sick to me.

Duane patted the top of Midnight's head. "Enjoy the luxury, because we're leaving in a few days. We're going back to Texas, and it'll be a lot of fun."

I'll bet.

It bothered Duane that his horse wasn't cooperative, but they hardly knew each other. Maybe I should trade him for another horse, because he's going to be trouble all the way to Edgeville. The snap of straw beneath a boot came to Duane's ears, and he went for his Colt. "Who's there?"

A vaquero appeared between two horses on the far side of the stable. "Don't shoot, amigo."

Duane holstered his gun. "You shouldn't creep up on people that way. I nearly shot your lights out."

"But I work here, Señor. I am Mendoza the stable-man, and I was listening to you talk with your horse."

"I don't think that he likes me."

"He is mostly wild, and will run away if he gets the chance." Mendoza glanced around suspiciously. "Be on your guard, because everybody knows who you are."

Duane felt electrified, as his hand dropped onto the walnut grip of his Colt. "What do you mean?"

"You were recognized at the cantina, and someone might want the price on your head. Perhaps it is time for you to hit the trail, senor."

"Thanks for telling me," said Duane, "and by the way, why *are* you telling me?"

"Because an *hombre* who talks with his horse cannot be all bad."

Duane looked over his shoulder for the bounty hunter lurking in the shadows. I'm worth more dead than alive, and I'd better get the hell out of here pronto, but a man needs a change of clothes, his bedroll, and extra cartridges for his Colt, just in case.

He drew the loaded pistol, headed for the front door of the stable, and looked both ways. Then he made his way toward the hacienda, the gun in his right hand, ready to fire.

Sheriff J. T. Sturgis dined alone at his personal table against the back wall of the Last Chance Saloon. The establishment was nearly empty, for most of the drunks still were in bed, sleeping off their night's adventures. But Sheriff J. T. Sturgis didn't touch a drop, and some folks believed that was part of his problem. But he didn't give a damn what others thought, because God had spoken to him in the Bloody Angle, and he knew what must be done.

His platter was covered with eggs, beans, bacon, and steamed tortillas, while a huge mug of coffee sent thin wisps of steam into the air. He continually looked around, because a trigger-happy kid might try to shoot the sheriff of Escondido to make his reputation as a dangerous killer.

Sometimes J.T. thought the Devil had defeated God, because the world was so wicked. The average man'll do anything for money, he believed, while the average woman can't be trusted. If these people think I'm going into hiding when the Pecos Kid comes to town, they've got another think coming. No kill-crazy cowboy is going to bamboozle J. T. Sturgis and get away with it.

Sheriff Sturgis had heard many stories about Duane Braddock since he'd become sheriff. Braddock had kicked the stuffing out of a few people, shot some others, and brought law and order to a town that never had seen law and order before. Braddock had broken the law himself a few times, but the city fathers looked the other way. Then the army had showed up, and the Pecos Kid had hightailed to Mexico.

If Duane Braddock comes to town, I'll take him the polite way, decided J. T. Sturgis. But if he goes for his gun, I'll blow his fuckin' head off.

Duane entered his bedroom, drew his gun, and stalked sideways to the window, where he placed his back against the wall. Slowly, carefully, he peered through the curtain. Nobody was in the courtyard hoping to catch the Pecos Kid.

He took his bedroll out of the closet, then stuffed his extra clothes into the saddlebags. He opened the door and nearly collided with Don Carlos coming from the opposite direction.

"Going somewhere?" asked Don Carlos, an expression of surprise on his face.

"On my way to Texas," Duane replied, keeping his eyes glued on Don Carlos's hands.

"So soon? But your leg is barely healed, and aren't you going to the funeral?"

"Certain people know my true identity, and I'm worried about my own funeral."

Don Carlos smiled. "But my dear fellow, you are under my protection, and the protection of Don Patricio. We are the law, and no one will touch you as long as you are with us. Of course, if you continue to visit the cantina . . ." Don Carlos shrugged. "I cannot protect you in the cantina, but Doña Consuelo would consider it an insult to her mother's memory if you left before the funeral. The poor girl is greatly distressed."

Duane felt awkward with bedroll and saddlebags, sneaking out the back door like a thief. "It's safer to travel at night," he acknowledged, "and if I waited till then, that would give me time to attend the funeral."

"Good — I'll see you there."

Duane returned to the bedroom, looked at his worried features in the mirror, and thought of seeing Doña Consuelo again. I'll be a perfect gentleman and a credit to my country whenever she's around, he vowed. I will not, under any circumstances, make improper advances.

One of Maggie O'Day's bodyguards approached Sheriff J. T. Sturgis in the Last Chance Saloon. "Maggie wants to palaver with you, Sheriff," he said.

Sturgis didn't want to hurry to the office and make it appear that he was Maggie O'Day's lapdog. So he rolled a cigarette and took a few puffs before arising. I wonder what she wants, he asked himself as he strolled down the corridor. At her door, he knocked and waited impatiently.

"Come in."

She sat behind her desk, puffing a cigar, a cup of coffee laced with whiskey nearby. He dropped to a chair in front of her. "Heard you want to talk with me."

She looked him up and down, then flicked ash off the end of her cigar. "I'll come right to the point. It's my understandin' that you mean to arrest Duane Braddock when he comes to town."

"That's right," admitted Sturgis. "I've got a pile of warrants for his arrest, and it's my job to bring him in."

"Not any more," she replied, looking him straight in the eye. "Yer fired as of right now. Hand in yer badge, and I'll pay you off, cash on the barrelhead."

She opened a drawer, took out a bag of coins, and counted his salary. He was dumbfounded that she'd fire him just like that. "But . . ."

"There ain't no buts," she told him evenly. "Duane Braddock was our sheriff at a time when there was two or three killin's every night. You don't appreciate what he did, although he made yer job a damned sight easier. If we had to choose betwixt him and you, we'd pick him every time."

Maggie was president of the town council, and had the authority to boot his ass out the door. "It's hard to believe that you'd fire me just fer doin' my job, ma'am. Somehow it don't seem fair."

"You work for us — we don't work for you. If you want to arrest the man that saved this town, you'd better start a-movin' on."

"But he's wanted by the federal marshal in San Antonio *plus* the Fourth Cavalry."

She leaned forward. "Fuck the federal marshal in San Antonio, and fuck the Fourth Cavalry."

"But he's killed people all over West Texas!"

"Maybe they deserved to die — you ever think of it that way? I know fer a fact that the galoots he shot in Escondido had no reason to go on a-livin', 'cause they was killers themselves. Listen to me, sheriff. Duane Braddock and I spent many a night in this very office, a-drinkin' whisky and a-shootin' the shit, and I probably know him better'n anybody. He's not the outlaw that people say, and everybody who knows him'll tell you the same damn thang. The lawyers will clear Duane Braddock eventually, if there's any justice in Texas, but if you want to stick yer face into the mess, you'd better saddle yer horse and move to the next town, 'cause we don't need you no more. You don't have the authority to arrest nobody, as of right now."

The brave corporal smirked angrily. "Everybody wants law and order for other people, but not for themselves. From the dirty thievin' bluecoat president of the United States to the lowest cattle rustler in

155

the Last Chance Saloon, they all think they're above the law. But the law is the rawhide that holds society together, and without it, we'd be wild animals a-tearin' out each other's throats."

"The law should serve the people, not the other way around. You talk about the law as if you know what it is. Just because it's legal to lock a man in jail, that don't make it right."

"You should've been a lawyer, Maggie. You've got an answer for everything."

"If you want to remain sheriff of Escondido, you know what it takes."

He shook his head vehemently. "Sorry, but I'm not the crooked two-bit sheriff that you thought you hired." Calmly, he unpinned his beloved tin badge from his shirt, then tossed it onto her desk, where it clanged atop a mound of coins. "Shove it up your ass."

Maggie didn't bat an eyelash. She counted out one hundred dollars and pushed it to him. "Here's yer pay."

He scooped it across the desk and dropped it into his pocket. "Nobody appreciates an honest man," he said through clenched teeth. "This is some world that we live in."

"Yer a hard-assed son-of-a-bitch," she

replied, "but I guess you can't he'p it. You was probably borned that way."

Doña Consuelo de Rebozo stood at the edge of the grave, wearing a black dress with a black veil covering her tearstained face, as the priest intoned Latin prayers. Nearby hovered her husband and father, with other relatives, servants, and vaqueros surrounding the grave. An unpainted wooden coffin nailed shut lay beside the hole in the ground.

Doña Consuelo sobbed softly as the priest showered the coffin with holy water. Then a group of vaquero pallbearers lowered the box into the hole. Doña Consuelo wanted to dive onto the coffin and be with her mother forever, but instead stood stolidly and bit her trembling lower lip. She felt as if she'd neglected her mother, and hadn't been a good daughter. I was thinking about having fun while my mother was dying. What a depraved person I must be.

Doña Consuelo loathed herself thoroughly as vaqueros shoveled dirt onto the coffin. Her mother disappeared beneath the ground, while her father sniffled and sobbed, daubing his eyes with a lace handkerchief. Is it true? Doña Consuelo wondered. Has he been unfaithful to my mother, and was our family life a sham?

She'd heard rumors that wealthy men sometimes kept mistresses, but had never dreamed that her bald-headed, roly-poly father could do such a thing. And now that she thought of it, perhaps Don Carlos had a woman in town too? Maybe that's why he was exhausted all the time.

Consuelo's world had been tossed upside down, and she felt adrift on stormy seas. Anything is possible, she realized, as her eyes fell on a certain tall gringo cowboy in the crowd. It appeared that he kept glancing surreptitiously toward her, but she couldn't be sure at the distance.

She felt alone, abandoned, with no one to turn to. What does it all mean? she wondered, as her mother's coffin disappeared beneath clods of dirt. Perhaps I should enter a nunnery, do penance, and sing hymns. How can I live without my dear mother?

Doña Consuelo's eyes weren't playing tricks, because Duane Braddock actually was glancing at her sneakily from the corners of his eyes. What is it about her that drives me loco? he asked himself. She's just another woman, isn't she?

He compared her with those of her sex

at the funeral, and noticed that her waist was slimmer than most, while her hips had a more pleasing line. She wasn't short, but neither was she too tall. Her breastworks were more than she required, but he wouldn't consider them flawed by any means. He couldn't see her face beneath the dark veil, but imagined her full-lipped Spanish beauty. At the age of eighteen, he considered himself a connoisseur of women and a man of the world. She was a tempting sight for his cheating eyes.

Whoa, he said to himself. There you go again, having despicable thoughts about that poor woman, and her mother's not even cold in her grave. What's wrong with you, Duane Braddock? Why can't you be a decent cowboy?

Duane averted his eyes, and let them fall on Don Carlos de Rebozo standing at his wife's side. Now there's a real man, Duane conjectured, not a lost wandering kid like me. Don Carlos has accomplished great things in his life, he's a wealthy caudillo, and it's no wonder that she's in love with him. But you've got to admit that he's old enough to be her father, and aren't men supposed to be useless in bed when they get old?

He shook his head in despair. Here I am

plotting the seduction of a married woman at her mother's funeral. I ought to confess to the priest, except I don't have the courage. Doña Consuelo will visit the chapel during the next few days, as she mourns her mother's passing. Perhaps I can run into her there, and we can say goodbye before I leave. It's the courteous thing to do, and I don't have ulterior motives, right?

CHAPTER 6

Doña Consuelo paced back and forth in her bedroom, grinding her teeth together. She felt cut loose from her moorings, as if she were losing her mind. There was a knock on the door, then Teresa entered and curtsied. "You wanted to see me, Doña Señora."

Doña Consuelo came to a stop a few feet in front of Teresa, placed her hands on her hips, and said: "I've heard a certain rumor about my father. Is it true that he has a woman in town?"

Teresa's face drained of color. "I do not know what you are talking about, madam."

"I heard it from your own big mouth, only you didn't know I was listening. What is her name?"

"Please, madam — I do not want trouble."

"It is too late for that," Doña Consuelo replied sternly. "Tell me or else I will dismiss you from my service. I buried my mother this morning, and have no time for insolence."

Teresa had never seen her mistress in such a state. "Maybe you'd better lie down, Doña Consuelo."

"Doesn't the priest say that we should always tell the truth? I'm a grown woman, and I demand to know: who is my father's mistress?"

Teresa said nothing, her lips sealed by the greater fear of Don Patricio's wrath. A tear came to the bereaved daughter's eye as she collapsed into a nearby chair. Doña Consuelo covered her face with her hands, and sobbed softly.

It hurt Teresa to see the beautiful lady in misery. She knelt before her mistress and took her hands. "What do you care about your father's mistress? All men do it — that's the way they are. The trick is to do it back."

"Please, please tell me her name."

"Doña Consuelo, I am afraid of your father."

"I'll never admit that you told me, and everybody else knows anyway."

The maid nodded sagely. "That is correct, madam. There was a big fight one night between your mother and father."

"Where was I?"

"In your bedroom. You were just a little girl. I do not know how your mother found out, but she threatened to leave your father. He pleaded with her, and finally she gave in when your father insisted that you needed her."

Doña Consuelo's head was spinning as her life crumbled around her. I've lived a lie, she realized, and no wonder my mother was so sad. My father betrayed her all these years. "What is the woman's name? Please — woman to woman — tell me. I swear to God that nothing will happen to you."

Teresa crossed herself, then kissed her thumb. "Her name is Conchita."

Duane awakened and found himself staring at a stained-glass window. He sat straight up in the pew, and realized that he'd fallen asleep while waiting for Doña Consuelo to appear. What kind of man would attempt to seduce a married woman in church? he asked himself.

He scratched his head in befuddlement, then sidestepped out of the pew. A statue of the Virgin stood at the end, gazing at

163

heaven, her arms outstretched, illustrating her response to the angel who'd told her that she'd give birth to the Son of God. In the words of Luke, she seemed to be saying, ". . . *be it unto me according to thy word.*"

Duane dropped to his knees in front of the Virgin, crossed himself, and meditated upon the Holy Mother of God. This is what women are really like, he figured. They're all innocent like the Virgin Mary, and they want to be good wives and mothers, but then we lying bastards get our hands on them, and pretty soon they're harlots.

He heard a sound behind him, whipped out his Colt, and spun around. To his astonishment, Doña Consuelo stood before him, wearing her black dress and veil, like the statue of a saint. He realized that she'd come to the Virgin Mary to pray, so he receded into the shadows.

She knelt before the statue, and prayed on her rosary with deep devotion, unlike those who rattled beads noisily while thinking of a trip to the general store. She's turning to the Virgin for help, instead of the nearest cantina, where I'd go, admitted Duane.

She sobbed, her body quaked, and she

appeared in the deepest extremity. Duane wished he'd never come to the chapel, because it was embarrassing to see her private grief. He had taken a silent step to the door when she keeled over and collapsed onto the floor.

He rushed to her side. She lay on her back, one knee in the air, her black hair radiating in all directions, white as a sheet. "Doña Consuelo — are you all right?" He touched her cheek, and it was cool, but her pulse was strong.

Duane realized that he was holding her hand, and he couldn't help scrutinizing it more closely. She had strong fingers, unlike the long, delicate digits of Miss Vanessa Fontaine. Her eyelashes fluttered; then her eyes bugged out at the sight of him.

Guiltily, he let her hand drop. "Evidently you fainted while you were praying, Doña Consuelo."

She looked around, sat up, and appeared confused.

"May I help you?" He placed one arm around her waist, took her hand, and assisted her to the nearest pew. "Perhaps you'd better sit down."

He sounded sincere, and she was surprised to see him there. She'd stopped for a brief prayer, sickened by her father's cruelty toward her mother, and had passed out. "I'm all right now," she said in a wavering voice.

They sat inches away, their eyes glittering in the darkness. "Maybe you should go upstairs and lie down," he suggested. "I'll take you there, if you like."

"No, there's something I've got to do first." Doña Consuelo's eyes filled with tears, and she sobbed uncontrollably.

He placed his hand on her shoulder. "I'm sure that your mother is in a better place now."

"She's in heaven," Doña Consuelo replied, then blew her nose into the handkerchief. "Sorry, but this has been a very bad day for me. If only you knew what I've been through."

"I understand." He placed his hand on her shoulder, gave a little squeeze, and smiled.

She felt moved by his gesture, and believed that he really did care. "You're a strange boy," she said.

"People have been telling me that all my life."

She felt oddly at ease with him. "Are you really a desperado?" she inquired.

"Let me put it this way — if you always

turn the other cheek, like it says in the Bible, some folks'll slap you right into the ground."

Close up, he was quite appealing, except for a few nicks and scars on his face, and a certain leer in his eye. "Where do you live?" she asked.

"I sleep on the desert as a rule."

"Aren't you afraid of Apaches?"

He winked playfully. "Aren't you?"

"But I don't sleep on the desert."

"Maybe you should try it some time. It's sanctified beneath the stars."

"What if it rains?"

"Just crawl under your tarpaulin. And you'll never go hungry because food's all over the place. There's nothing like fresh antelope loin roasted over a mesquite fire."

He's a wild man, she thought, as she measured his well-proportioned limbs. "Do you intend to spend the rest of your life living like a *lobo?*"

"I plan to get married someday, but there's something I've got to do first."

"What's that?" she asked.

"It's personal. Sorry."

She looked at him askance. "I've never met anybody like you."

"I've never met anybody like you either,

Doña Consuelo. Your husband is a lucky man."

She laughed. "I'm not sure he would agree with you."

"But it's obvious how much he loves you."

She recalled something that she'd intended to do. "I've got to be going," she said. "Perhaps I'll see you at dinner?"

"I'm leaving at sundown," he replied.

"But you just arrived. You should rest your leg for a few more days, and perhaps we can talk again. You have an interesting point of view, and I don't often meet people with whom I can speak."

He bowed his head slightly. "Doña Consuelo, if I can be of service, I'll stay as long as your patience will tolerate me."

"Good — I'll look forward to talking with you."

She disappeared into the outside corridor, as Duane closed his eyes, his heart beating wildly. I think she likes me, he said to himself.

He dropped to his seat in the pew, scratched his chin, and wondered whether to saddle up old Midnight and cut out for Monterrey without delay. The air was filled with her fragrance, his head floated with desire, and a certain pesky artery throbbed in his throat. I'm in love with another man's wife, and it's got to be a disaster, he warned himself. But I promised I'd stay until she got tired of me, and a Christian is only as good as his word.

Doña Consuelo came to a stop before a squat adobe hut, as villagers in the vicinity became alarmed. One of them ran toward the hacienda, to warn Don Patricio, but Doña Consuelo had more important business at hand. She knocked on the door loudly. "Open up!"

The door fell ajar, and a short stout woman appeared. She had a moon face and wore a plain cotton dress. "Doña Consuelo," the woman said, bowing low.

Doña Consuelo walked into the tiny enclosed space. It had a stove, bed, dresser, and table in one room. "I understand that you are my father's mistress?"

Conchita was unable to speak, and Doña Consuelo felt a mad urge to whack her, when a little boy strolled wide-eyed into the room. Doña Consuelo lost her breath, because the child was the spitting image of her father, and even resembled Doña Consuelo herself.

Doña Consuelo dropped heavily onto one of the wooden chairs at the table. "It's true," she whispered, closing her eyes. "My God."

She felt Conchita's hand on her forearm. "I am sorry, Doña Consuelo. I did not mean disrespect to your mother, but your father offered many pesos, and I did not even have shoes. Now I have anything, with new dresses and my own home. Try to imagine yourself in my place, Doña Consuelo. What would you have done?"

No matter how hard Doña Consuelo tried, she couldn't imagine herself as a hungry peasant. "It's not your fault, I suppose. My father is to blame."

"Forgive him, for he is a good man. He was lonely, and it is not his fault."

"He had my mother, and she was the finest woman who ever lived!"

Conchita bowed. "Your mother was a saint, but your father had other needs, and that is why he came here. You are a married woman yourself, and surely you understand."

Doña Consuelo felt weak in the knees, while the little boy stared at her with big brown eyes. "My half-brother," she whispered in disbelief.

"The other little ones make fun of him," said Conchita, "because he has no father."

Tears welled in Doña Consuelo's eyes, as

the clear light of innocence shone in the boy's eyes. "What is your name?" she asked.

"Pepito," he replied.

Doña Consuelo wanted to scream at the top of her lungs, but couldn't hate a little boy. She removed the rosary from her neck and draped it around his. "From your sister," she said, then kissed him lightly.

The lady of the manor arose, turned toward her father's concubine, and said, "You and my brother will never lack anything as long as I am alive. If you need me, just go to the hacienda and ask for Doña Consuelo."

Conchita bowed her head in gratitude, as Doña Consuelo made her way toward the door. The crumbling poverty of the shack dispirited her, and she loathed her father thoroughly. A man of character would not do this, she told herself. I will not let him get away with it, so help me God.

The sun set over the rooftops of Escondido as J. T. Sturgis sat in his hotel room, counting coins. They totalled one hundred and sixty dollars, approximately what a cowboy earned in five months, more than enough to finance another trip to a different town that needed a lawman.

But Sturgis's abrupt dismissal still rankled deeply. He could ride on, but it wouldn't provide the same satisfaction as getting back at Maggie O'Day. Serve her right if I made a citizen's arrest and tossed Duane Braddock in jail. Hell, I'd be famous, they'd make me a federal marshal for sure, and no two-bit whorehouse madam could ever fire me again.

He dropped the coins into his left front pants pocket, then glanced at a picture of General Pickett displayed on the wall, next to a miniature Confederate flag. The bitter taste of defeat fouled the ex-corporal's mouth, and he wanted to exchange it for the sugar of victory. "If I came through Gettysburg," he muttered, "the Pecos Kid should be a piece of cake."

Doña Consuelo knocked on the door of her father's bedroom, and a manservant opened the door. "Is he here?" she asked.

The manservant bowed. "I'll see if he's available, Doña Señora."

"I'll look for him myself."

She marched into her father's suite of rooms, as the manservant stared at her aghast. "But Doña Señora . . ."

She ignored him and headed for her

father's private office. Without knocking, she flung open the door. He sat on an easy chair, sipping a glass of brandy, his shirt collar unbuttoned and cravat hanging askew. He appeared dazed, glassy-eyed, and distressed.

"What are you doing here?" he asked, trying to rise.

"I want to talk with you."

His features sagged, his eyes were red, and she realized that he'd been crying. "I'm not feeling well," he said in a low voice.

"Neither am I, because I've just found out the truth."

"What is Truth?" he asked dreamily, slurring his words. "Does anyone really know?"

"Conchita and Pepito are truth, Daddy."

He went pale, his jaw dropped open, and he fell loose on the chair. "You know," he said weakly.

"I've just met my half-brother, and he looks just like you. You're my father, and I will always love you, but I will never forgive you for this. Not only have you betrayed the most wonderful woman who ever lived, but you have also betrayed me, and made my life a travesty."

"It's true," he replied in a barely audible

voice. "I am the most despicable man who ever lived."

"I practically worshipped you," she continued, tears streaming down her cheeks. "I thought I had a wonderful father who loved my mother, but it was a lie. How could you do this to us?"

He couldn't look her in the eye. "Your mother was a saint, but I never claimed to be a priest. Your mother was —"

She wouldn't let him finish. "Don't you dare say another word about my mother! One day you'll have to answer for this, but I swear — I will never speak with you again!"

She opened the door violently. A group of servants had gathered in the corridor, listening to the battle royale. "What are you doing here?" she asked. "Have you no work to do?"

She pushed them imperiously out of her way as she headed toward the stairs that led to her husband's chambers. Don Carlos has been part of the silent conspiracy against me, and I wouldn't be surprised if he has a fat little peasant woman in a filthy little hut somewhere, and *that's* why he's never home. These lying cheating damned men — you can't trust any of them, and when they tell you they love you, that's when you've got to watch them the closest.

The cantina was dark, smoky, and filled with vaqueros, and everyone looked at Duane Braddock as he neared the bar, his black hat slanted low over his eyes. "A bottle of mescal," he said to the man in the apron.

"*Sí*, Señor."

The bottle appeared, and Duane spun around suddenly to make sure no bounty hunter was aiming a shotgun at the center of his back. He flipped a few coins on the bar, tucked the bottle beneath his arm, and watched everybody's hands as he headed for the door.

The clear night air smacked him in the face. He wondered where to go with the bottle, because he didn't want to get drunk alone in his room. He stopped in the lee of a hut, pulled the cork, and took a swig. It went down like velvet, warmed his belly, and enlivened his mind. What's wrong with me? he asked himself. I hid in church to seduce a married woman who was in *mourning*, and if that's not enough, I'm becoming a drunkard like all the other banditos and vaqueros.

He shrugged sadly as he recalled the

innocent young acolyte singing in the monastery choir. I used to be a decent God-fearing Catholic, but now I've committed every sin in the book, and if that's not enough, I'm chasing a married woman.

He came to the edge of town, where an endless expanse of cactus slept in the moonlight. Maybe I should go to confession, because Christ said that he loved repentant sinners. I'm ready to get down on my knees and beg his forgiveness, but first I'd better have one last shot. He stopped, tossed back his head, and took another swallow.

Don Carlos sat on his balcony, smoked a cigarillo, and gazed at the desert sprawled before him. The death and funeral of his mother-in-law kept him from important business matters, and he wondered how many more days he'd have to stay at the Vásquez hacienda.

The end of the cigarillo glowed cherry red, while in the village someone strummed a mournful guitar. If Don Patricio died, Don Carlos would inherit the Vásquez holdings, and become one of the wealthiest landowners in Mexico.

Don Carlos wanted to sire a dynasty that would live forever, but unfortunately his wife had not yet conceived. Sometimes he thought about marrying a more fertile woman, but he loved Doña Consuelo, in his haughty caudillo way. Perhaps in a few years I'll leave her, he speculated, although he knew that he could never give up his sweet little Doña Consuelo.

He was startled by the door bursting open behind him. "But Doña Señora —" said one of the Carlos's bodyguards.

"Out of my way!"

Don Carlos arose from his chair as his wife stormed into the parlor, face blotched with emotion, hair wild in all directions, a mad glimmer in her eyes. She came to a stop in front of him, crossed her arms, and said, "I know everything."

He couldn't help smiling, because she looked like an angry little girl. "About what?"

"My father and the woman in town."

Don Carlos was amazed that she knew. "I hope you're not going to say anything."

"I told my father that he's a pig, but God will have to forgive him, not me. This might come as a shock to you, my dear husband, but I don't like it when people lie to me. We're husband and wife, yet you never saw fit to tell me the truth."

"What good would it do?"

"Do you have a woman in town too?"

"You're all the woman I can manage, Doña Consuelo, and I'm perfectly happy with you."

"I'm sure my father said the same words to my mother, and it appears that I have a half-brother too. I no longer respect my father, and want to leave this place at once."

"But darling — it would be a terrible insult to your father."

"My father has insulted my mother and me, and deserves to be insulted back."

"But Doña Consuelo — a man has his needs."

"What are these *needs* that everybody keeps talking about? If my mother didn't want to sleep with him, and I don't blame her, now that I think about it, he should've remained faithful to the marriage anyway, and to me."

He smiled wryly. "Is it *your* vanity that's hurt, and this has nothing to do with your mother?"

Doña Consuelo was taken aback by the charge. "It has everything to do with my mother. What are you suggesting?"

"You're meddling in your parents' marriage, which is none of your business, and evidently you've been making a public spectacle of yourself. Perhaps you'd better lie down and get some rest. You're becoming overwrought."

"My father is a traitor, and all you fine gentlemen lie constantly, although it's always the woman's fault. How soon can we leave this place?"

"Twenty-four hours. Anything less would be indecent."

"Was it decent for my father to break my mother's heart?"

"I suspect it's *your* heart that you're worried about, my dear."

She backhanded him across the face so suddenly, he didn't even see it coming. He took a step backwards, as his face smarted. "Stay away from me," she replied, as she rushed toward the door. "I want to be alone."

Duane staggered across the desert, holding the half-empty bottle in his right hand, hat on the back of his head. What is a man except a hank of hair, a few pints of blood, and his Colt .44? he asked himself.

The Milky Way blazed across the sky, and he spotted the Cassiopeia constellation, the Lady in the Chair. Why do women drive men loco? Duane asked himself. Why don't we all get married and have babies as God commanded us, instead of behaving like a bunch of yard dogs?

He shook his head in dismay. Only a depraved individual would attempt the seduction of a married woman in church. I baited the hook with sincerity, but all I wanted was to take off her clothes.

He felt mortified, sickened, and disgusted with himself. I should ride to the monastery, apologize to the abbot, confess my sins, and live the holy life again. If I continue in my present direction, I'll spend eternity in hell.

He stopped, gasped, and dropped to his knees. Yes, that's it, he decided. It's back to the monastery for me, but I can't let this mescal go to waste. He raised the bottle, kissed its lips, and took another healthy swallow. The desert whizzed around him like a cactus carousel, as he raised his eyes to the incandescent heavens.

"Forgive me, oh God, for I have sinned," he whispered. "I feel lost, I'm choking on my sins, and do you think you could possibly give me a sign, to tell me what to do?"

Hozen the Apache crouched behind a jumble of paddle cactus, holding his knife in his right hand, the calves of his legs poised to attack the white eyes who knelt twenty paces away. It was a stroke of good fortune, for Hozen had come to the village to steal a rifle, but instead the white eyes had come to him like a gift from *Yusn,* the Great Spirit.

It appeared that the white eyes was drunk, as Hozen noted the pistol, holster, and gunbelt full of ammunition. The clothes would fit, and perhaps even the boots, not to mention the hat. Hozen had no money to buy such articles, because Apaches had no general stores or armament factories. If a warrior wanted a gun, he had to steal it.

The white eyes pitched onto his face, evidently out cold. It's almost too easy, thought Hozen, as he dropped onto his stomach. Then he crawled forward with his knife in his teeth, on his evening shopping tour.

The former seminarian wasn't unconscious; he lay in mild religious ecstasy, sniffing the aroma of the earth as his mind reeled through the caverns of time. A great civilization lived here once, he told himself, but it was swallowed by the Spanish Conquest. And one day perhaps the

United States of America will be gone, although it's hard to imagine. Yet the Toltecs, Olmecs, Aztecs, and Mayans thought their cultures would endure forever too.

His finely-tuned ears heard a knee scraping gently against a clump of grama grass. He turned, and his eyes widened at the sight of an Apache warrior leaping toward him, knife aimed at his gizzard!

Duane grabbed the Apache's wrist with his left hand, then punched him solidly in the mouth with his right. The blow caught the Apache coming in and snapped his head back, but he recovered quickly, and struggled to ram the knife into Duane's heart, as Duane grasped the Apache's throat.

The Apache wrapped his free fingers around Duane's arm, flung himself backwards, somersaulted, and kicked into the air. Duane was thrown off him, landed on his back, and hopped to his feet. The Apache was charging again. Duane reached for his Colt, thumbed back the hammer, and pulled the trigger.

Click. It was a misfire, and the Apache slashed his blade at Duane's nose. Duane leaned backward, then brought the gun up and crashed it into the Apache's face, laying flesh open to the bone. The Apache lost consciousness as Duane pulled the trigger of the next cartridge. *Click*. Two in a row, an almost unheard-of calamity, and all Duane could do was pass it to his left hand for use as a club, while he yanked his own Apache knife from its scabbard.

Meanwhile, Hozen found himself in more of a fight than he'd anticipated. He jumped to his feet and wondered whether to run, but then noted the pistol, clothes, and boots, and his eyes glimmered with greed. He believed that any Apache could defeat any white eyes on any day of the week, so he took a deep breath, gripped his knife tightly, and charged once more.

Duane dodged to the side as he aimed the point of his knife toward the Apache's throat. The Apache feinted to the left, feinted to the right, and then lunged forward, streaking his sharp point toward Duane's midsection. Duane pivoted, ripped his knife across the Apache's wrist, severing countless tendons, and then, on the backswing, slit the Apache's jugular.

Duane landed a few feet away as the Apache stood confused in the moonlight, his throat gushing blood. He seemed not to know what had hit him; then his eyes became glazed, and he crashed to the ground. Duane gulped air, trying to recover his equilibrium, for the attack had been sudden, silent, and during an intense moment of prayer.

Duane knelt beside the dead Apache and rolled him onto his back. The Apache had gone to the happy hunting grounds, an expression of astonishment on his face. Duane worried that all his cartridges were defective, then heard a sound, dropped silently onto his belly, and cocked the hammer, hoping the next cartridge was a winner. He took aim at a figure approaching through the thicket, but no Apache would make such noise.

It was a woman wearing a shawl, and she looked like an apparition in the moonlight. He didn't want to scare her, but she was wandering aimlessly more or less toward him. A ray of moonlight fell onto her face, and it was Doña Consuelo de Rebozo.

Duane didn't know whether to jump for joy or curse his bad fortune. *I've tried to get away from her, nearly got killed by this Apache, and now here she is again. Lead me not into temptation, but deliver me from evil.* She appeared to be sleepwalking, or in one of those strange moods that women sometimes have.

"Doña Consuelo — are you all right?"

he asked gently.

Her face froze into a mask of trepidation. "Who's there?"

"Duane Braddock."

"My God!" She touched her hand to her heart. "What are you doing here?"

"Just taking a walk, but it's not a very safe place, I've just found out." He aimed his revolver at the dead Apache. "You shouldn't be here without your bodyguards."

Her cheeks were ivory in the pale light, while her eyes glowed like burning coals. Her black hair framed her face, while her shawl made her look like the Madonna of Guadalupe. "What's wrong with him?"

"Lead poisoning."

She stared at Duane for a few moments, then gazed at the dead Apache. It was the weirdest day of her life, and she was ready for anything. She scrutinized Duane Braddock's youthful features, but he didn't appear capable of killing a fly. "I think I'm going mad," she said in an odd sing-song voice. "Do you think I could sit down?"

"Right this way," he replied, as though in his living room. He led her to a nearby clearing surrounded by thorny foliage. "Have a seat."

The ground was hard-packed dirt and

grama grass, and they both sat cross-legged opposite each other. They didn't speak for a long time, as night birds squawked and a lone *lobo* continued his desert serenade.

Finally Doña Consuelo said: "What would you do if everything you believed in turned out false?"

He shrugged, grinned, and said, "I'd try to get on with my life."

"Have you ever been betrayed by someone you loved?"

"Once," he admitted. "I fell in love, we were supposed to get married, but she ran off with somebody else. I still can't get over it, to tell you the truth."

"That's the way I feel." She lowered her head. "I thought I had a certain life, but it was a lie. It turns out that my father betrayed my mother, and my husband is probably betraying me. I hate both of them, and I'll never trust another man as long as I live."

"I'd never trust another woman," retorted Duane. "It's a funny thing about love. People say they love you, and a few days later they're chasing somebody else."

"But there are some people who fall in love once, and stay in love for the rest of their lives. That's the kind of love I thought my parents had, but what a delusion it was. I've met my father's woman, and I've got a half-brother too. I don't have proof on my husband yet, but I'm sure I'll find out if I try."

Duane pulled the brim of his hat low, so she couldn't see his roving eyes. She's not getting along with her husband. Hmmmm. He reached into his back pocket. "Care for a drink?"

She stared at the bottle. "What is it?"

"Mescal. And it's not bad considering what I paid for it."

She wrinkled her pretty nose. "I could never drink that."

"It might relax you."

"I don't want to relax. I want to *do* something."

"Like what?"

"Kill my father, or my husband. Or maybe I should kill myself, and get it over with."

He held out the bottle. "Have some mescal."

She narrowed her eyes, trying to comprehend the strange creature sitting before her. He's half-drunk, he's just killed an Apache, but there's something nice about him. "I don't know if it's a good time for me to drink mescal," she said.

"On the other hand, it might be the best time of all."

The bottle dangled before her, and he appeared priest-like, although his latest victim lay less than a hundred paces away. She reached for the bottle. "I need something after what I've been through today, and maybe this is it."

She took a sip, coughed immediately, and turned red. Duane patted her gently on the back. "Easy now," he said, thoroughly repelled by his own behavior. Here I am getting her drunk so I can seduce her, but why can't I stop myself?

"What terrible stuff," she said, making a face. "How can you tolerate it?"

"As far as I'm concerned, mescal is the greatest gift that Mexico has given the world."

"I feel so confused — I don't know what to do."

"When I get confused, I try to remember something an old friend told me. 'A soldier keeps advancing toward his objective, despite wounds, hunger, illness, doubt, fear, or whatever.' "

"Perhaps I should leave my husband, because he was part of the lie. I feel as if he's cheating on me."

Duane glanced around, holding his

revolver ready to fire. "We'd better start back to the hacienda. There's no telling what's on the desert tonight."

They arose and stood inches apart, the moon outlining them with silver. She looked up at him, and he gazed down at her. Their eyes met, and he felt drawn to her.

"Oh, Duane," she said with a sob, "I'm so lost."

She embraced him, placed her cheek on his chest, and absorbed his strength and warmth.

"I know what you're saying," replied Duane, as he comforted her with roaming hands. "I've been lost all my life, but after a while you get used to it."

"Sometimes I don't believe there's a God."

"My main problem is I'm a sinner, and can't seem to stop."

"You don't seem so terrible to me."

"But you can't see my mind."

"I'm sure it's not *that* bad."

She became aware that she was belly to belly with a handsome athletic young man, and his hands were on her rear end. "You're right — we'd better go back to the hacienda," she told him. "There may be more Apaches in the vicinity."

He couldn't let go, as though she were a magnet and he mere iron shavings. "Doña Consuelo — may I tell you something?"

His request took her by surprise. "What is it?"

"I'm leaving first thing in the morning, and I just thought I should say that you're one of the loveliest people I've ever met in my life."

It was silent, as they gazed into each other's eyes. A falcon flew overhead, and the *lobo* in the distance barked at the moon. Doña Consuelo felt pure desert energy bolt through her, but was frightened and hopeful at the same time. "I think you're very decent too, Duane."

They were confused young people living at the extremes, and somehow, as if by magic, they were prompted to hold each other more tightly. "Oh, Duane — I'm so unhappy."

"Me, too," he replied. "Nothing I do ever turns out right, and I live like that *lobo* on the ridgeline. God, it gets lonely sometimes."

"I don't have anybody to talk with," she confessed, "although I'm constantly surrounded by people. My father treats me like an idiot, and so does my husband, while everybody else is dishonest. I may not be lonely, but I'm certainly alone."

They clutched each other as if each were the other's life preserver, and he felt her body heat radiate through their garments. Intoxicated by her splendor, he tried to remind himself that she was a married lady, and he a former Benedictine monk.

Meanwhile, she was aware of his taut body, so different from Don Carlos's corset. "My God," she breathed, as his devilish fingers found her right breast. The sensations were new, wonderful, and her head was dizzy from that swallow of mescal. Their lips touched lightly, she smelled the desert emanate from his being, instead of her husband's French cologne. What am I doing? she asked herself.

His lips pressed more insistently, while his hand caressed her maddeningly. She knew that she should push him away, but her world had collapsed that day, and her brain was aflame with desire. She had nothing to hang onto, so she abandoned herself completely to his soothing ministrations. It felt as though she were melting in his strong arms, and his passion literally swept her off her feet.

He lowered her gently to the ground, and feasted like a vampire on her throat. She's mine! he thought triumphantly, and her body was real flesh and blood, unlike that of the skinny and prissy Miss Vanessa Fontaine. He lay atop her. Their lips touched, mouths opened, and surreptitiously, he raised the hem of her gown.

The tips of their tongues wrestled gently, and she knew that she was far over the edge. They rolled across grama grass and anthills, groping at each other's clothing. A twinge of shame swept through him, followed by a wave of pleasure as his hand came to rest against her bare leg.

Delicious electricity zapped through her, and never, not even in the early nights of her marriage, had she known such lunacy. She tingled in every membrane, and a tiny soft sugary explosion caused her to growl low in her throat.

Her voice roused him to further excess, as he removed the remainder of her dress. Doña Consuelo de Rebozo, the beautiful and elegant young Spanish noblewoman, lay naked before him, her eyes glittering as though somebody had lit a bonfire inside her skull.

He undressed quickly, their warm writhing bodies came together, and at that point, nothing could stop Duane, not a tribe of Apaches, not an earthquake, not even Don Carlos with a double-barreled shotgun in his hand. She scratched her fingers across his back, their teeth ground together as Aztec drums pounded in their ears, and they coupled desperately in the moonlight.

Where the hell is she? wondered Don Carlos, as he paced back and forth in his bedroom. He cursed and sputtered, because he hated to be impeded by unnecessary problems. Goddamned women — whenever there's trouble, they come apart at the seams.

Doña Consuelo had not gone to bed like a dutiful little wife, and Don Carlos wondered where she was hiding. She's an emotional child, he considered, and she might do something foolish, like shoot herself. At first he'd found her jealousy amusing, but now her erratic behavior was getting on his nerves.

There was a knock on the door, then García entered the bedroom. "She is nowhere in the hacienda, sir."

The nobleman's eyebrows raised in surprise. "Wake up all the men, search the village, and if she's not there, comb the desert. I'm afraid that Doña Consuelo is distraught, and may do something foolish."

The vaquero departed, and then Don

Carlos walked to the balcony, where he stood with hands on the rail, the cigarillo sticking out of his teeth, eyes probing the desert before him. He'd thought she'd be in the library or her mother's bedroom, but it appeared that she'd taken leave of her senses altogether. You can't predict female behavior, he thought cynically. Just when you've got them figured out, they confound you yet again.

It had been a shock when she'd called him a liar to his face. If she'd been a man, he would've challenged her to a duel. Don Carlos couldn't understand why she was angry, because keeping a mistress on the side was a common pastime among men of his class. When Don Carlos had been married to his first wife, he'd maintained several women over the years — and Maria had understood completely, as long as she was queen of the hacienda.

Don Carlos hoped that Doña Consuelo hadn't wandered onto the desert, out of her head. I'll have to sit her down and give her a stern lecture when she gets back, he said to himself. I can't have my wife behaving like a madwoman in front of the servants.

Miss Vanessa Fontaine was experiencing

heart palpitations in the dressing room of the Last Chance Saloon. I must be coming down with something, she told herself, as she took a sip of whiskey from a glass next to pots of cosmetics on her dressing table.

She'd felt unpleasant twinges since arriving for work that night, as if the world were off-kilter. Must be getting old, she determined, as she applied a dab of rouge to each glorious cheekbone.

There was a knock on the door. "Time to go on, Miss Fontaine," said one of Maggie's bodyguards.

"I'll be right there," she answered as she applied the final touches to her professional mask. Every night it takes a little longer, she acknowledged. I'll be thirty-two soon, so what am I doing throwing my life away for a man who's probably forgotten me? For all I know, he could be screwing another woman right now.

She arose from the dressing table, removed her apron, and studied herself in the full-length mirror. She wore a evening dress of black Chambéry gauze with gold-colored stripes, a square neck, and appliqué embroidery of silk and chenille on tulle. In the darkness, she could see the former Charleston belle looking back at her, but with new confidence and maturity in her eyes. I'm as good as I ever was, she tried to convince herself, and who knows, maybe tonight *he'll* be in the audience. With a rustle of skirts, she turned melodramatically and headed for her first performance of the evening.

Duane and Doña Consuelo put on their clothes, aware that they'd both passed the boundaries into a fearsome new world. The experience had been so stupendous, they were speechless. Duane strapped on his Colt, positioned the holster for a fast draw, and then tied the leather thong on the bottom of the holster to his leg.

"What now?" she asked, a faraway tone in her voice.

"Damned if I know."

They hugged, and she pressed her lips against his chest. "I'm in love with you — I think."

He buried his face in her fragrant black hair. "If this isn't love, what is?"

My life will never be the same, she cogitated, as she felt his warmth against her face. How can I go back to my husband? Catholic guilt smacked her in the face, and she shuddered uncontrollably.

"You're cold," he said. "We'd better get back to the hacienda."

"Not yet — please."

He couldn't take his hands off her, and wished they could be in a nice safe bedroom, because there were many more acts that he wanted to perform, but even young people must be prudent on the desert. "It's dangerous here, Doña Consuelo."

"We've got to talk."

Oh-oh, he thought. They always want to talk. "What's wrong?"

"I don't love my husband, and I'm not going to live with him anymore. Why don't you take me with you?"

"You can't be serious!"

"After what has happened with us, how can I go back to Don Carlos?"

"But the U.S. Army is after me, and I'm constantly on the run. Perhaps you'd better give this more thought."

"I made the assumption that . . ." Her voice trailed off.

"The assumption that I loved you?" he replied. "But I do, and if you want to come with me, I could have no finer or more beautiful woman than Doña Consuelo, but you can't bring your maids with you, your clothes might get a little raggedy, and you could end up in jail. Just because I'm innocent, that might not save *you* from the hangman's noose."

"If you love me as I love you, I will follow you anywhere."

"We could run out of water, and you won't believe the rattlesnakes in some of those canyons. Sometimes wild pigs attack for the hell of it. And there's something I haven't explained yet. I'm on my way to —"

"I don't care where you're going, as long as I come with you."

She clasped him more tightly, and his hands happened to fall on her glorious rump. This is a fabulous woman, and they don't come along every day, he considered. If she's willing to play the game, I'll give her a run for her money — why the hell not? "When do you want to leave?"

"Right now."

"You'll need a coat, a blanket, and a gun. If there's one thing I've learned, it's don't go running off half-cocked. We must make plans, gather what we need, and leave after everything has settled down. Surprise is the most important element of attack, as one of my old soldier friends used to say."

She didn't want to return to the house of lies, but could appreciate common sense when she heard it. "Very well," she agreed. "We will do it your way."

He heard something. "Get down."

She dropped to her knees, as a voice called: "Doña Consuelo!"

"They're searching for me," she said.

"Go to them, and we'll meet in the library around three o'clock tomorrow afternoon, to see how everything's going."

She peered into his eyes. "Just tell me something. You really do love me, don't you?"

"We're meant for each other, otherwise we could not have done what just happened. Now you'd better get going before they find me."

He helped her rise, rippled his tongue against hers, and eased her toward the vaqueros. "Doña Consuelo!" they called.

"I'm here!"

She blew Duane one last kiss, then turned toward the vaqueros. Duane slunk back into the shadows and watched her recede into the night. What a woman! he thought. My God, I've actually done it with Doña Consuelo de Rebozo! He couldn't believe his great good fortune. It just goes to show you that if you say your prayers every night, all good things will come to you.

He heard a vaquero say: "So here you are, Doña Consuelo. Your husband has been worried about you."

"I was taking a walk," she replied.

Duane smiled cynically in the shadows of the moon. They're all actresses, he meditated, and we men are a bunch of lying varmints. I'll spend eternity in the hottest oven they've got, after what I just did, but I have no regrets. It was beyond anything I've ever known, except Miss Vanessa Fontaine.

It all came back to Miss Vanessa Fontaine. Even now, in the aftermath of love with another woman, he couldn't help reflecting upon the former Charleston belle. Passion with her had been like seeing the face of God, but she'd deserted him for somebody else, and Duane was certain that Doña Consuelo de Rebozo would do the same. You can't trust any of them, he warned himself. I'll bet she changes her mind by the time tomorrow night rolls around.

"She has been found, sir."

"Has she been hurt?"

"No, sir. She is on her way here now."

The vaquero closed the door, leaving Don Carlos alone. The nobleman crossed himself and gave thanks to the sacred heart of Jesus. I mustn't be angry, he counseled himself. She's no more than a child, and she's just buried her mother, who was being betrayed by her father. It might take a few days before she returns to normal.

There was a knock on the door, and suddenly she entered, wearing a dress that looked as if she'd been rolling in the dirt. "What happened to you?" he asked.

"I took a walk, became sleepy, and lay on the ground. It was restful, and I fell asleep."

"You're lucky an Apache didn't kidnap you."

"I would hardly consider myself a lucky person, after today. Anyway, I apologize for losing my temper earlier, but you know how much I loved my mother. If you don't mind, I'll need my own room until my year of mourning is over."

"I understand, of course," he replied with a little bow. There was something different about her, and it wasn't just her dirty dress and the blush on her cheeks, as if she were wearing rouge. No, she had a confidence and presence that he'd never seen before. This is how death can bring maturity to a woman, he considered. "I hope you're not going to chastise your father further. He's been drinking heavily ever since you raked him over the coals."

"I hope he drinks himself to death," she

said levelly, "and now, if you'll excuse me, I'd like to take that bath."

Doña Consuelo walked toward the door like Carlota, former Empress of Mexico, instead of a humble nun rattling her rosary beads. It's time she grew up, Don Carlos decided, as she departed in a swirl of dirty skirts. There was something sluttish on her smudged features that he liked. Perhaps, after a decent period of mourning . . .

Duane returned to the hacienda by a side entrance, and moved silently toward his room, as the black bat of Catholic guilt followed wherever he went. I poured mescal down a married woman's throat, and whispered sweet nothings into her ear. Then, when she didn't know where she was, I tore off her clothes and practically raped her. My God, what's wrong with me?

He entered his room, crossed to the balcony, and gazed at the star-spangled sky. I should be locked in prison where I can't harm innocent women, he admonished himself. But he had to admit, despite his wicked, wicked ways, it had been a great pleasure. And besides, he cogitated, she really didn't drink that much, and I meant every word I said. No one could say that I forced her, and if she were happily married, it never would've happened in the first place. What have I *really* done wrong?

The more women Duane met, the less he understood them. They were always irrational, in his estimation. Doña Consuelo de Rebozo, a religious married woman, had lain naked on the desert with a drifter and outlaw whom she barely knew.

Am I really in love with her? he asked himself. But it doesn't matter, because in the cold light of day, with her maids waiting on her, she's not riding off into the desert with the likes of me. Women are loco, but they're not *that* loco.

Ex-sheriff J. T. Sturgis leaned against the back wall of the Last Chance Saloon, and observed a performance by Miss Vanessa Fontaine. He noted that her every movement was calculated to produce an effect, and each eye in the house watched avidly, as she manipulated them cleverly.

Sturgis couldn't help admiring her skill at casting a spell over the audience. If I didn't know better, I'd be in awe of her too, he admitted. She knows the good old songs, but she's just as bad as any common criminal, and if she gives me any backtalk, after I arrest the Pecos Kid, I'll lock her ass in jail too.

He imagined her in a cell, wearing rags, a frightened glint in her eyes. You fool all the others, but you don't fool me, Miss Vanessa Fontaine. One of these days, I'm a-gonna show you that the law is the law. God punishes the wicked, and judgment day is a-comin' down on all of us.

Doña Consuelo lay amid steamy bubbles, her eyes closed, as warm water soothed the tissues of her body. She felt as though she'd been wrestling a wildcat, and couldn't believe some of the acts she'd performed with him.

I'm going to pay heavily for this, she thought fatalistically. I've dishonored my family and shown how weak my faith really is. But I'm in love with that Americano, or in lust with him, and can't think straight anymore.

Paradoxically, she'd never been so happy, excited and ecstatic, and she couldn't wait to see him again. How sinful can it be? she asked a painting of the Virgin. It would be different if I had children. I never should've married Don Carlos, but how could I know that one day Duane Braddock would come along?

She wished he could be in the tub with her, and they could soap each other. He must love me too, she believed, otherwise he wouldn't have done all those marvelous things. No, that's not something you can pretend. It frightened her to know that she'd developed a deep compelling need for him. Yes, I'll run away with him to the ends of the earth, and the devil take the hindmost.

In the light of recent events, she viewed her father differently. He cheated on his spouse because he needed something, and so did I. Now she understood the weaknesses of the flesh, and couldn't help feeling sorry for her father. My mother should've been a nun, and Daddy should've married somebody else. Maybe God doesn't care about the petty things we do, as long as we don't hurt each other too badly. A new swamp of guilt engulfed her. My poor father is suffering because of me, and I'm no better than an alley cat.

She emerged from the tub, maids toweled her gently, and she put on a blue silk sleeping gown, then a white velvet hooded robe. She made her way down the corridor to her father's bedroom, a chill came over her, and she feared that he'd killed himself over her cruel insults.

An additional ton of guilt fell over her, and she staggered beneath the weight. The poor man — how he must have suffered from my false sanctimonious pride. She closed her eyes and uttered: "Lord, I hope that nothing has happened to him."

She knocked on the door, there was no answer, and she turned the knob. The room was dark, her father slouched in a chair, a bottle of brandy and a glass on the low mahogany table before him. She lit a lamp, and was shocked by his disarray, with his shirt half-unbuttoned, a stain on his pants, and a ghostly pallor on his cheeks. He looked as though he were wallowing in the lower depths of hell.

"Daddy," she said. "Can you hear me?" His eyelashes fluttered vaguely, as she knelt before him, taking his hand in hers. "Daddy, I'm sorry for what I said earlier. We're all weak vessels, and if I told you some of the things I've done recently, you'd never believe it."

He didn't say anything, but a tear appeared at the corner of his eye. A sob escaped his lips, as he reached for his daughter. They embraced, and Doña Consuelo had the strange feeling that her mother was hovering above, as the family of sinners became reconciled.

Don Carlos de Rebozo sat on his terrace,

smoked a cigarillo, and let his mind wander. The night desert spread before him, dark and ominous, the ancestral homeland of the Apache, now populated with Don Patricio's cattle and other holdings. Don Carlos often didn't sleep well, and spent many nights pacing, thinking, and dreaming.

Sometimes he reflected upon Seville, home of his ancestors. Don Carlos could trace his history to the Moorish invasion, and it gave him pride to know that he was descended from knights in the service of the crown. One of them, Don Diego de Rebozo, had come to America with Cortés, to gain his fortune in the strange new land. Don Diego had battled Indians, but the Spanish conquerors had been altered forever by Indian culture, and together they'd built modern Mexico.

Don Carlos had visited Seville in his teens, after crossing the Atlantic in a tall-masted Spanish galleon. He'd loved the vistas of Andalusia, and had revelled in the sheer elegance of the Spanish court, but after a few years he'd missed the iridescent hues of Mexico, its tempestuous people, and rides on the open range, accompanied by his laughing, guitar-playing vaqueros.

There was a knock on his door, and he

hoped it was Doña Consuelo asking to spend the night. The doorknob turned, but it was García. "May I speak with you alone, sir?"

"By all means."

García entered the bedroom and closed the door. "Don Carlos," he said respectfully, "there is something that you should know. It may have no importance, and I might be wrong to bring it to your attention, but . . . the gringo was seen returning from the desert a little while ago, and . . . his clothes were very dirty."

The vaquero backed out of the room, and Don Carlos wrinkled his nose in confusion. So what if . . . Suddenly it hit him. No, it can't be, he said to himself, as his lungs deflated sickeningly. She wouldn't, she couldn't, it's impossible, but they were on the desert at the same time. Had they been rolling in the dirt together?

The mere thought nearly drove him to his knees. He knew from personal experience that Doña Consuelo was a hot tamale once you got her going, while Duane Braddock was the type of lazy useless fool that women generally adored. Were they actually screwing on the desert like wild animals? A sharp pain arose in Don Carlos's chest, and he dropped into the nearest upholstered chair.

It can't be, but on the other hand, they both were wandering in the wilderness at the same time, and you wouldn't expect them to come back hand in hand. No, they'd split up, but isn't it interesting that they both looked like they'd been wrestling with somebody? His heart beat faster, and he broke into a cold sweat. Did my dearly beloved wife dishonor me and my family with that reckless young killer? Don Carlos de Rebozo imagined the armored knights of Seville gazing at him from the sky, their swords outstretched. I won't jump to conclusions, he warned himself, but if I find evidence that she in fact has committed this foul deed, I would not hesitate to kill them both.

Duane sat cross-legged on the floor of his bedchamber, and held the Colt .44 to his head. Pull the trigger and get it over, he said to himself. After what you've done, you don't deserve to live.

He didn't want to die, but couldn't tolerate himself. No matter how you look at it, I enticed a married woman to sin. The priests and brothers warned about the sins of the flesh, but I didn't pay sufficient attention.

He was concerned that Doña Consuelo would go berserk and confess everything to her husband. If I had any sense, he lectured himself, I'd pack my saddlebags and hit the trail *pronto*. I'm sure she's not going anywhere with me, after she thinks it over. Then he recalled the rapture of her naked undulating body. But if she did, I'd be the happiest man in the world.

CHAPTER 7

Doña Consuelo located a closet filled with pistols, rifles, holsters, and boxes of ammunition. Most of the weapons were gifts to her father, with handles wrought from silver, ivory, and gold. She didn't know one gun from another, but found a lethal-appearing length of iron that looked like Duane's, then strapped on a brown leather holster, covered everything with her shawl, and was on her way to breakfast.

She'd heard scandalous stories about women leaving their husbands for adventurers, and now it was her turn. Her family would disown her, but she could never again sleep with Don Carlos. God had sent Duane Braddock to me for a reason, and she couldn't turn her back on love.

She thought perhaps she'd gone mad, for

she was running off with a strange American outlaw. She wanted to lay naked in his arms, drink mescal, and have fun for a change, before she ended in Lucifer's bean stew.

She entered the dining room, and saw *him* eating eggs, tortillas, bacon, and beans heartily. He glanced at her, smiled uncertainly, then returned to his breakfast with gusto. The eyes of her husband followed her as she walked toward the seat opposite him.

"How are you this morning, my dear?" he asked pleasantly.

"Quite well," she replied.

"I didn't sleep last night, and neither did our guest. But a woman can sleep through anything."

"Not always."

What did she mean by that? Don Carlos asked himself. He glanced at Braddock, who methodically devoured everything in sight. I remember when I had a healthy appetite, Don Carlos mused. A terrible desolation came over Don Carlos, and he slouched at the table.

Doña Consuelo glanced at her husband as she elegantly downed her breakfast. In the morning light, the lines and ravages of his tanned visage were cruelly indicative of his age. I fell in love with a fairy tale, she realized. He's older than my father, and treats me like an idiot child.

She noticed Duane finishing his last swallow of coffee. He wiped his mouth with his napkin, smiled broadly, and said: "Think I'll take a walk."

He strolled from the room, and his spurs jangled down the hall.

"When did he say he was leaving?" asked Don Carlos.

"He didn't mention anything that I recall," replied Doña Consuelo.

Don Carlos knew that he was being a jealous fool, but couldn't stop himself. "What do you think of him?"

"I hardly know him."

"Would you consider him attractive?"

"What an odd question."

Don Carlos realized that it truly was an odd question, and regretted asking it. "Just curious," he said, with a choked little laugh. "You seem different since you've returned from the desert last night. Has anything happened?"

"I've forgiven my father for lying."

"I'm glad to hear it, and it might be best if we left as soon as possible. How about tomorrow morning?"

"So soon?"

"Is there something keeping you here?"

"Such as?"

He smiled. "Concern for your father, of course."

"You're right — he'll be better off alone. If you want to leave tomorrow morning, I'll notify the servants."

In the library, Duane found volumes of history, novels, works of poetry, philosophy, science, and theology. It didn't take long to locate *The Imitation of Christ*, by Thomas à Kempis. It was a book that he'd studied at the monastery, and he carried it to the table, opened it at random like a roulette wheel, and saw:

Firstly, be peaceful yourself, and thus you will bring peace to your fellows. A man of peace does more good than a very learned man.

It's true, he preached to himself. I should dwell in that quiet gentle part of my heart, but unfortunately I can't find it any more. He glanced toward the next page:

. . . to be able to live at peace among hard, obstinate, and undisciplined people, plus those who oppose us, is a great grace and a

most commendable and manly achieve-ment.

Anyone can be a lowdown son-of-a-bitch, considered Duane, but it takes a real man to stay relaxed when most folks are angry, vengeful, and spiteful. If I had any sense, I'd start building my own ranch, so I wouldn't have to tolerate other people's bad manners. Then I'll marry the right woman, and live like a decent Christian for a change. He flipped a few more pages and saw:

Whoever clings to any creature will fall with its falling; but he who holds to Jesus shall stand firm forever.

Maybe so, pondered Duane, but I can't live without pretty women. He recalled his all-too-brief interlude with Doña Consuelo, and his ears became warm. I hope she shows up, because I'd love to get my hands on her again.

Not every desire comes of the Holy Ghost, though it may seem right and good; for it is often difficult to judge whether a desire springs from good or evil inclinations, or whether it arises from your own selfishness.

Many are deceived in the end, who at first seemed to be led by the Holy Ghost.

The door to the library opened, and Doña Consuelo materialized, dressed in black like the Madonna of death. "Oh, hello Duane," she said, as if they hadn't plotted the rendezvous.

"Howdy," he replied nonchalantly. "Fancy seeing you here."

"I felt like reading something, to take my mind off things." She selected a tome, joined him at the table, and opened it. "What are you reading?" she asked.

"*The Imitation of Christ.* How about you?"

"*Don Quixote.*"

"I studied it at the monastery," explained Duane. "My favorite character was Sancho Panza." He looked both ways, then lowered his voice. "Have you changed your mind?"

"About what?" she whispered.

"Coming with me."

"Why would I change my mind?"

"You're giving up an awful lot."

"When you ask certain questions, I think you don't feel as I do."

"I can't believe you'll really run off with me."

"That is because you don't see yourself as I do." She reached beneath her black shawl, yanked the gun out of its holster, and lay it on the table. It was a Colt .44, just like his, but with gold inlaid custom grips and apparently never fired.

"Maybe you'd better put it away before somebody sees it," said Duane. "Do you think you can make it to the barn around midnight without being seen?"

"No, because they watch me closely. However, there is one place where they will never follow — the house of my father's woman, Conchita, I will visit her and my baby brother late this afternoon, just before nightfall. You will be waiting behind her home with a horse for yourself and another for me. We will leave then, and no one will miss us for a long time, I hope."

He analyzed her plan, studied its frail edges, and tried to poke a hole through the center. "Where will I get the second horse?"

"You'll buy it from Don Carlos, and he might even give it to you. You'll need a packhorse, won't you?"

"I don't have that many things to pack."

"Lie," she said, as the Devil giggled victoriously in a corner of the library.

"I hope your husband doesn't suspect

anything," uttered Duane.

"I think he does, actually. We must be careful, and we shouldn't be seen together again until tonight."

They pursed lips and kissed long-distance. Then she arose, returned the book to its spot on the shelf, and walked in measured steps to the door. He undressed her with his eyes, and recalled grappling with her on the desert. I can't believe, when it comes right down to it, that she'll be at Conchita's tonight, he told himself. Cowboys like me aren't *that* lucky.

Doña Consuelo walked the corridors of the hacienda, passing sofas, chairs, and tables holding bowls of ripe fruit. She felt relieved and at peace with her decision, although she feared deadly consequences. But what is life without love? she wondered. And what does it profit a woman if she gains a fortune but loses her soul?

My marriage was inspired by convenience, while I, little Doña Consuelo, got lost in the shuffle. She relived the wrestling match with Duane Braddock's firm strong body, the scent of desert in his hair, and his all-engulfing passion that had transported her to the pinnacle of ecstasy. I can't live without him, and I don't know what'll happen to me, but maybe we'll get married one day, after we make the proper contribution to the right bishop.

Don Patricio sat in his office, the top button of his shirt unfastened, his cravat untied and hanging loose. A bottle of Spanish brandy sat on the table, next to a goblet made from cut glass. The landowner hadn't shaved since the funeral, and a foul reek emanated from his body, as he looked at Don Carlos through bloodshot eyes. "I apologize for not being more hospitable . . ." began Don Patricio.

"I understand, of course," replied Don Carlos, standing before him. "I've come to tell you that Doña Consuelo and I shall leave first thing in the morning."

"Go with God, my friend. I hope that our next meeting will be under happier circumstances."

Don Carlos retreated from the office, anxious to be alone with his thoughts. Jealousy nagged him mercilessly, and he wondered what to believe. Is Doña Consuelo having a love affair with Duane Braddock behind my back?

Suddenly the Pecos Kid appeared around the corner of the corridor, a big friendly smile on his face. "Just the person

I'm looking for," he said.

Don Carlos smiled back falsely. "What can I do for you?"

Duane hitched his thumbs in his belt and peered into Don Carlos's eyes. "I've decided to hit the trail first thing in the morning, and I'd like to buy a horse."

"What's wrong with the one you have?"

"I need another for a packhorse."

Don Carlos raised his hands generously. "You may have whichever horse you like. Nothing is too good for the man who saved my wife's life."

They shook hands. "If I don't see you before I leave," said Duane, "thanks for the hospitality."

Duane receded down the corridor, and Don Carlos envied his youth, vitality, and undeniable good looks. The old nobleman felt a twinge of jealousy, although Duane Braddock was a callow young man, in his estimation. *Is he putting the horns on me?* wondered the caudillo.

Don Carlos de Rebozo knew there was no honor among men where women were concerned, and even blood brothers sometimes stole each other's wives. *Duane Braddock just looked me straight in the eye, but if I were sleeping with his wife, I'd do the same thing.*

Don Carlos knew the wickedness that dwells in the hearts of men, because he'd seduced other men's wives as a devil-may-care student in Seville. Once his limbs had been as sound as Duane Braddock's, and he'd climbed balconies to be with his ladies, who themselves were deceiving husbands or fathers.

Don Carlos knew that proper religious ladies like Doña Consuelo could be the most outrageous once they broke with Holy Mother Church. He removed a lace handkerchief from his pocket and mopped the slick of sweat on his brow, overwhelmed by disgraceful and unworthy considerations. The vaqueros are probably laughing behind my back, he feared.

He turned the corner, and nearly bumped into García. "I have something to tell you, sir," the captain of vaqueros said solemnly.

Now what? Don Carlos asked himself. "Out with it, and don't spare my feelings."

"A dead Apache has been found in the desert. Evidently he came to raid last night, but someone killed him with a knife."

"Perhaps the Apaches were fighting among themselves."

"There were boot tracks just like the gringo's."

Irony tinged García's answer, and it wasn't lost on the nobleman. It would explain why Braddock was dirty and ragged when he returned from the desert, but on the other hand, it proved that he was there at the same time as Doña Consuelo. Perhaps they'd met before or after Braddock killed the Apache?

Don Carlos was getting a headache from so much speculation. "I'll be in my room, if you learn additional information."

García bowed, as Don Carlos proceeded to his chambers. He removed a bottle of brandy from a cabinet, poured a stiff drink, and gulped it down. Events were moving too quickly, and he didn't know what to believe.

He sat on the balcony chair, and was just getting comfortable when the door opened. It was Doña Consuelo, an angry expression on her face. With great effort, the great man arose to greet his possibly errant wife.

"What are you doing to me?" she began indignantly. "Why am I being followed everywhere by your vaqueros? Do they think I'm going to run into the desert?"

"I have no idea . . ." he lied, backed

against the wall.

"Tell them to stay away from me. Understand?"

"I will give the orders right now. García!"

"He is coming," replied a voice on the other side of the balcony.

Doña Consuelo's eyes were narrowed with barely concealed rage. "If I see one more of those hounds behind me, I'll fire him."

"But Doña Consuelo . . ."

She didn't reply, and Don Carlos speculated that her magical transformation was taking a turn for the worse. They heard running footsteps, then García turned the corner. "You wanted to see me, sir?"

"Yes," replied Don Carlos, "I —"

Doña Consuelo interrupted him. "I'll give the orders, if you don't mind, my dear husband." She turned slowly toward García, who shriveled beneath her merciless glare.

"García, hereafter you and your men will stop following me, and if I catch them up to their old tricks, they and their families, and you and your family, will no longer be employed by us. Do I make myself clear?"

García bowed in terror. "Yes, Doña Consuelo."

The vaquero backed around the corner, as Don Carlos studied his wife with new interest. Never could he imagine such words coming out of Doña Consuelo's mouth. She reminded him of titled ladies whom he'd met in Seville, who'd managed immense households as El Cid had commanded his army in the battle for Valencia. "You've frightened poor García," he said with a forced chuckle.

"Excellent," she replied, "because that was my intention. I'm going to town later in the day, and may not be back for dinner."

Hesitant about asking, he did so anyway. "Why are you going to town?"

"I want to spend time with my new brother before we leave, if you don't mind."

"Don't you think there'll be a scandal?"

She raised her eyebrows in scorn. "My father's infidelities are practically an institution, and everybody has accepted them except me. But the boy is part of my family, and I'd like to give him a little present. It is not proper for a Vásquez to live like that."

"I'm certain that your father will make new arrangements, now that your mother has . . . departed."

"I think that Conchita and Pepito should move into the hacienda. There's plenty of room, and the boy should receive an education, don't you agree?"

"Absolutely, your royal highness. My, how you've changed these past few days, Doña Consuelo. I've never seen such a conversion in my life. What has happened to you?"

"I'm in mourning for my mother, and I'd like to be alone."

"Don't forget that we're leaving first thing in the morning."

"I'll get to bed early," she replied. "I promise."

Duane cleaned his Winchester, then loaded it with seventeen cartridges. He ran a patch down the barrel of his Colt .44, blew out the chambers, and cleaned dust from little crannies with a brush that he'd bought in Escondido, his last stop in the good old U.S. of A.

He packed his saddlebags, noting that he was low on ammunition, and that one of his shirts was getting threadbare. We'll have to buy supplies in the first town, he reminded himself. He counted his funds, approximately two hundred American dollars in coins.

He felt like a rich man, but the desert was full of Apaches. He doubted that Doña Consuelo would adapt to life on the dodge, but told himself not to worry. She's not running away with me, because she's not that stupid.

There was a knock on the door, and Don Carlos made his grand entrance. "Ah, you're packing," he said. "I'm glad I've caught you." He held out a leather bag the size of a grapefruit. "This is for you, from Don Patricio and me."

Duane opened the bag, and his eyes bugged at the sight of gold coins, approximately two thousand dollars worth. "I don't deserve it," he said, "but I sure as hell won't turn it down."

Don Carlos couldn't help smiling. He's just the kind of lost rake that women love. They want to save him from himself, or at least that's what the little vixens tell themselves, but what they really want is his . . .

Duane Braddock held out his hand. "Thanks for everything, sir. You've been real good to me."

Their hands embraced, as they performed the ancient ritual. Don Carlos peered into Duane's eyes, and said, out of the blue: "Tell me something, Mister Braddock. I can't help wondering — are you having a love affair with my wife?"

Duane's eyes dilated, and he noted the position of the cuckold's hands. "I may be a wanted man, but I'm not *that* bad," he said.

Don Carlos realized the enormity of what he'd just admitted to a strange gringo, but couldn't stop. "Sometimes even the most elegant ladies surrender their dear little hearts to utter scoundrels."

Duane smiled. "I guess there's no telling what goes on in a woman's mind."

"Sometimes I wonder if they have minds in the first place." The difficult moment passed, and Don Carlos took the opportunity to retreat. "Have a safe journey, my friend," he said, as he made his way toward the door.

Don Carlos traversed the corridor, wondering if Duane Braddock was romancing Doña Consuelo in the nooks and crannies of the hacienda, as he, Don Carlos, had done in Seville, when he'd clambered across treacherous rooftops to reach the boudoirs of certain ladies.

You can't put anything past young lovers, Don Carlos admitted ruefully. Nothing keeps them apart, once they make their minds up, and isn't it clever how Doña Consuelo arranged for the vaqueros to stop guarding her?

The caudillo could place his wife in shackles and chains, declare her insane, and transport her back to his hacienda, where she'd be under guard for the rest of her life, but he'd been a young cavalier once, had fought duels over matters of honor, and would have contempt for any man who'd lock up his wife.

She's a grown woman, Don Carlos acknowledged. If she wants to leave me, I wouldn't stop her. But Doña Consuelo has too much dignity to take up with a low-class gringo, no?

But Don Carlos had been viewed as a low-class provincial himself when he'd arrived in Seville nearly forty years ago. Many fine titled ladies who should have known better had admitted him to their beds, because the sad truth was that even the most exquisite women were attracted to wastrels and outlaws. Perhaps they need somebody to look down upon, speculated the man of the world. They probably say to themselves: *He's such a fool, he couldn't possibly judge me.*

Don Patricio saw his daughter standing before him, wearing a black shawl. "I need some money, father."

228

"What in the world for?"

"Personal reasons."

"Why don't you ask your husband?"

"Because I'm asking you."

She looked like the Madonna of death in her black shawl, and he shivered involuntarily. "In my office, the bottom drawer on my desk — take whatever you need."

She kissed his forehead. "Thank you, Daddy, and whatever happens — I'll always love you."

He smiled at the touch of her lips, and then she was out the door. She located the appropriate drawer, and her eyes widened at the sight of gold coins five inches deep covering the bottom. She scooped handfuls into the big pockets of her suede skirt. Her father snored as she slipped toward the door, glanced both ways, and headed swiftly toward the village.

Duane gazed into the eyes of his unfaithful horse. "How's it going, pardner?" he asked cheerfully.

It was going all right before you came along, Midnight seemed to reply, chomping oats.

Duane looked him over, and the animal appeared to have put on a few pounds. "Sure doesn't look like you've missed any meals while you were here."

I've got a feeling I'll be missing some soon, Midnight blinked sorrowfully.

Mendoza appeared out of the shadows. "You are going somewhere, señor?"

"Moving on," replied Duane. "Don Carlos said I could take any horse I wanted, in addition to my own — you hear about that?"

The stablemaster bowed at the mention of the great caudillo's name. "Those were Don Carlos's orders, sir."

Duane leaned toward the stablemaster and confided out the corner of his mouth, "What's the best horse here?"

"Best in what way, señor?"

"Endurance, speed, and fairly easy to handle. A horse a woman might like." He winked. "I've got a girlfriend in another town, and I'd like to take her with me."

"You want a gentle horse, but a gentle horse will not run as fast as a wild horse."

"I want the fastest gentle horse you've got."

"That is Josephina."

"Make sure her shoes are in good condition, then saddle her for a long trip. I plan to leave soon as it gets dark."

Hiding behind a grandfather clock, Don

Carlos watched Doña Consuelo pass down the corridor. His heart ached violently, because formerly she'd found any excuse to be with him, and seemed to crave his attention, but now she dined alone in her room, and was leading a life that had nothing to do with him.

What is she up to? he wondered, as he slipped silently across the shadows. Is she really going to town, or has she planned to meet Duane Braddock in the hayloft? He maintained a discreet distance, peered through the lower corner of a window, and saw her headed for the village, head held high, unlike the whiny, simple-minded former Doña Consuelo.

He was tempted to run after her, but managed to control himself. Doña Consuelo would never leave me, he decided, because she's got too much to lose.

Duane sat on Midnight's back and gazed at twinkling village lights at the edge of town. Beside him was Josephina, who kept casting sidelong glances at Midnight, while that great beast snorted and snuffled in annoyance at Duane sitting upon him again. I ought to toss him into the air, thought Midnight darkly.

"Relax," Duane said. "What the hell's wrong with you?"

Midnight shook his head from side to side. I'm tired of your ridiculous and dangerous shenanigans.

"Come on — you're my horse, I stole you with my own two hands, and if you keep up your rotten goddamned temper, I'll get rid of you first chance I get."

Duane peered at the back of Conchita's house, waiting for the lantern to pass in front of the rear window, the signal for him to bring Josephina. Doña Consuelo will never go through with it, he anticipated. I'm wasting my time, but it won't hurt to have an extra horse in case this damned Midnight gets too persnickety.

Doña Consuelo knocked on the door, and it was opened by Conchita, who immediately bowed. "Doña Consuelo," she said. "I am so surprised to see you."

Doña Consuelo wore a brown suede shirt, red silk blouse, suede jacket, and wide-brimmed vaquero sombrero. "This is the last time I'll bother you, I promise," she replied, as she entered the small enclosed space. "Where is Pepito?"

"Asleep."

"May I see him?"

Conchita led Doña Consuelo to the corner, where Pepito slumbered in a box filled with straw. Doña Consuelo knelt beside the makeshift bed and whispered: "You carry the blood of the Spanish nobility in your veins, little brother." Then she withdrew a handful of coins from her pocket, and passed them to Conchita. "Take this, and buy him new clothes. I have spoken with my father, and you will move into the hacienda before long. Pepito will have his own tutor, and become an educated man. It is possible that my father will marry you someday."

Conchita stared at her wide-eyed. "Married? The hacienda? Me?"

"I'm leaving," Doña Consuelo said. "I don't know what's going to happen, but tell my father that I'll always love him, and kiss Pepito every day for me."

Doña Consuelo lifted the lamp off the table, carried it to the rear window, and passed the light back and forth three times.

"Who are you signalling?" asked Conchita. "Are you sure you're all right?"

Doña Consuelo heard approaching hoof-beats, and a tremor of fear passed through her. "I apologize for being cruel last time I was here, my dear stepmother. Now perhaps I am a little wiser, and I must follow my destiny wherever it leads."

Doña Consuelo hugged the short peasant woman, then kissed her cheek. Horses' hooves could be heard approaching the rear of the hut, and Doña Consuelo hesitated for a moment, but only for a moment, then reached for the door.

In the backyard, the Pecos Kid sat atop a black horse. "Howdy," he said like a rough old cowboy, his hat slanted at a rakish angle, hand resting on his gun, and his sharp eyes glancing about nervously. "Coming along for the ride?"

Doña Consuelo placed her foot in Josephina's stirrup, and raised herself into the saddle. Midnight pranced sideways, anxious to get rolling, but Duane held him on short rein, as he leaned toward Doña Consuelo.

"Are you sure you want to go through with this?"

"We'd better start moving, before someone realizes that I've gone."

He spurred Midnight, who walked softly toward the desert. Josephina followed, carrying Doña Consuelo away from family, reputation, and social acceptability. The noblewoman turned toward the hacienda, lights burned in long corridors, and she felt a twinge of sorrow. They passed darkened shacks at the edge of town, and soon found themselves in the wilderness. It closed around them, and the town couldn't be seen behind heaps of vines, cactus, and scraggly desert trees. After a short distance, Duane steered Midnight into a gully and brought him to a halt.

"What is wrong?" asked Doña Consuelo, coming abreast of him.

He held out his hand. "Hand me your gun carefully, please."

She passed it to him, and he proceeded to examine it, noting that it was a Colt like his, except for the fancy Mexican handiwork. "You ever shoot one of these?" he asked, as he loaded it.

"Not yet."

"Just thumb back the hammer, pull the trigger, and get ready for the kick. If we run into Apaches, save the last one for yourself." He loaded the gun with five cartridges, leaving the hammer resting on the empty sixth chamber.

She swallowed hard, as she accepted the gun. "I don't know if I could do that."

"Let's hope we don't put it to the test. By the way, it's still not too late to turn back."

She scowled. "Sometimes I think that you don't want me along."

"We'll travel all night, because we want to put as much distance as possible between us and your husband. Before sunup, I'll find a place for us to sleep. Are you with me?"

"Absolutely," she replied.

He leaned toward her, kissed her lips, and their tongues touched lightly. Then, reluctantly, they parted. Duane wheeled Midnight toward the Sierra Madre Mountains, and gave him a nudge with his spurs. The horses advanced deeper into the night, merged with the shadows, and disappeared.

CHAPTER 8

Don Carlos sat at the dining table and wondered why Doña Consuelo hadn't joined him for breakfast. They were scheduled to depart for their hacienda that morning, but evidently she was sleeping late, while Don Patricio remained drunk in his bedchamber, muttering to himself.

Don Carlos drank his second cup of coffee, musing about his beloved wife. He viewed her as the fountain of youth itself, and the mere thought of her never failed to revive him. I'd better wake her up, he thought with a smile, as he finished the coffee. His amorous mood heightened by caffeine, he launched himself down the corridor and up the stairs to her door. He knocked, anxious to see her in her night clothes, loose and sleepy, susceptible to salacious promptings.

No one stirred on the other side of the door. She must *really* be asleep, poor child, thought Don Carlos, as he opened the door. The bed was made, and she was nowhere in sight. "Doña Consuelo?" He rushed to the next room, where she took baths, but the tub was empty and dry as a bone. Don Carlos's jaw dropped open, his heart pumped noisily, a terrible horror came over him, and he struggled to understand. Wait a minute, he cautioned himself. Perhaps she arose early and has gone for a walk. "García!"

"He is coming, Don Carlos," called a voice.

Don Carlos opened the closet, and her beautiful dresses hung cheek by jowl. He touched the white lace of a black velvet dress, one of her favorites. He raised the sleeve to his nostrils to catch her scent.

Footsteps entered the bedchamber, and Don Carlos dropped the sleeve immediately. García strode toward him, the usual hangdog expression on his face. "You wanted to see me, Don Carlos?"

"Where is Doña Consuelo?"

García shrugged. "I do not know, sir. None of us want to lose our jobs, but . . ." He looked both ways, then said, "Gonzalez saw her walking toward the village late yesterday afternoon. What is wrong with Doña Consuelo, sir? Has she gone loco?"

Don Carlos realized that his wife was embarrassing him, an intolerable situation for a caudillo. He placed one fist on his hip, scowled, and said, "Round up the vaqueros and search for Doña Consuelo. Do you know where her maids are?"

"No, sir."

"Find them, and send them here at once."

García rushed out of the room as Don Carlos gazed at the empty connubial bed. It occurred to him that he might never sleep with Doña Consuelo again, and all his worst fears were coming true. He dropped onto a chair, lit a cigarillo, and tried to think clearly.

She wouldn't give up her ancestry, would she? he asked himself. But wait a minute, she's probably in the library, her favorite spot, or the chapel. I'm letting my fears run away with me.

He arose from the chair, and was on his way to the library when Teresa, his wife's chief maid, approached from the opposite direction. "You wanted to see me, sir?"

"Do you know where Doña Consuelo is?"

"No, sir."

"Why aren't you attending to her?"

"Yesterday afternoon she said she wanted to be alone, so she could mourn her mother in peace."

"Who made her bed this morning?"

"Not me, and neither did any of the other maids."

"You may return to the servant's quarters," Don Carlos said stiffly.

Don Carlos walked back to his rooms, sat in a dark corner, and pondered the unused bed. Where did she spend last night? The sun rose in the sky, but it was gloomy and nebulous in Don Carlos's heart. Where is my wife?

Duane Braddock lay on the crest of a hill and gazed though his C.S.A. brass spyglass at a scattering of buildings on either side of the trail. It was barely a village, and he wondered if they had a store that sold cartridges for Colts, a blanket for Doña Consuelo, and some tarpaulin to keep her dry in rainstorms.

But somebody might recognize the Pecos Kid, and there could be gunplay. He clambered down the hill, where Doña Consuelo was waiting at the bottom with the Colt in her hand.

"It's a little town," he explained. "We

have to buy some things, but be ready to ride at a moment's notice."

She climbed onto her horse, and rode closer to him. "When are we going to stop for a rest?"

"After supper. Your husband might be on our trail, and we can't take chances."

"I will never go back to him," she declared, as if she really meant it.

But Duane still didn't trust her, because she'd been pampered all her life. A few days of this and she'll change her mind, he was certain. "Stay close, and watch out for drunken vaqueros. Some of them come to town after a few months on the range, and they haven't seen a woman for so long — they go loco. I should give you shooting lessons, but there isn't time. If there's trouble, drop to the floor and don't get up until I say so."

García said: "We have looked everywhere, sir. She cannot be found."

"You must have overlooked something," replied Don Carlos. "Did you search the barn?"

"I have told you, sir, that we have looked everywhere."

"But a person cannot simply disappear."

"We have learned that Doña Consuelo

has visited Conchita and given her some money. There were fresh hoofprints behind Conchita's house, and Conchita could not explain why they were there."

"How many horses?" asked Don Carlos. "Two."

"And you followed the tracks?"

"They led into the desert."

"Please leave me alone."

The door closed, and Don Carlos slouched in his chair like a sack of beans. Then he arose, hooted like a bull, and smashed his fist into the wall, nearly breaking his hand. I am dishonored, he thought, and this can only be settled in blood. He looked at himself in the mirror, as his lips quivered with rage. They cannot get away with this as long as there is breath in my body. "García!"

The door opened, and the sad-eyed chief of vaqueros stood there. "Sir?"

"It appears that Doña Consuelo has run off with the gringo. Round up the men, and load a wagon with supplies. Don't forget dynamite, because there might be trouble."

The normally reticent vaquero appeared surprised. "But . . . how many days will we be out, sir?"

"As long as it takes to bring back Doña

Consuelo, but I don't think they've gone far. See if you can find an Apache who knows how to track, and hire him. I'll pay one thousand dollars in gold to the man who brings back Doña Consuelo alive!"

Duane and Doña Consuelo rode down the main street of the village, alert for trouble. A few vaqueros strolled dirt sidewalks, children played merrily in an alley, and a wagon was being loaded in front of the store. There was also a stable and cantina. "Seems safe enough," uttered Duane.

All Doña Consuelo could do was follow the Pecos Kid. They stopped in front of the rail, tied up their horses, and glanced around cautiously. "I'll do the talking," said Duane. He strolled toward the door, then glanced behind him suddenly, in case a lost wandering lawman had spotted him. Then he opened the door and stepped out of the backlight, ready to draw and fire.

Two vaqueros conversed with the proprietor, who stood behind the counter, working on their purchase order. The proprietor raised his eyes and gazed through thick spectacles at the newcomers. "May I help you?"

"I'd like to buy some cartridges for a Colt .44, a blanket, a warm sweater for my wife, a shirt for myself, a tarpaulin, and some food."

"Matilda!" called the proprietor.

A sturdy middle-aged woman with Indian features appeared from behind the curtain.

"Take care of these customers."

Duane repeated his order, and then Matilda pored through the shelves. The proprietor scratched his pen on the order as one of the vaqueros roved his eyes up and down Consuelo's curves. A grin came to his grizzled lumpy face, and he said, in a voice barely above a whisper. "Señorita — why do you go with a boy, when you can have a man?"

Doña Consuelo had never been spoken to in such a tone, and she looked at the man as if he'd just crawled out of a rathole. Meanwhile, Duane measured the vaquero carefully, because an insult had clearly been leveled, and according to the unwritten law of the region, massive retaliation was in order. But Duane didn't want trouble in a strange land, and decided to let the incident pass, noting that the vaquero had been drinking, and was unsteady on his feet.

"What are you looking at, gringo?" asked the vaquero.

Duane wanted to ignore him, but the orphan acolyte loathed bullies. "You're digging your grave with your mouth," he replied.

The vaquero stiffened. "Gringo, perhaps you want to impress your woman, but you had better be careful what you say, or I will kill you."

The other vaquero stepped between them, trying to smile. "Let us relax, my friends. There is no reason to fight, because fighting never proves everything."

"Out of the way," ordered the other vaquero, as he lunged for his iron.

Duane smacked his Colt, and it fired before his opponent's barrel cleared its holster. The small store filled with smoke, and the vaquero was struck center chest. He coughed drily, and then dropped in a clump to the floor, where a pool of blood widened around him.

Duane flicked his gun barrel toward the other vaquero. "I'm not looking for trouble."

The vaquero raised his hands. "Neither am I, Señor."

Matilda placed the merchandise on the counter while Doña Consuelo stared at the corpse on the floor. She'd never seen a killing, and its suddenness had thrown her into shock. Duane counted out the coins, then filled his saddlebags with fresh cartridges. The proprietor wrote out a bill of sale, Duane pocketed it, then gathered up the remaining merchandise.

"*Vámonos,*" he said to Doña Consuelo.

As if in a dream, she followed him out the door. Duane was gratified to find their horses still tied to the rail. He chucked the saddlebags onto Midnight, while Doña Consuelo climbed into her saddle.

They wheeled their horses, touched spurs to the animals' withers, and galloped down the street, kicking up clods of muck, as residents gazed at them from behind windows. "*Adiós,* amigos!" shouted the Pecos Kid, waving his hat over his head, as he and his dazed consort disappeared over the first rise.

In the general store, the remaining vaquero, whose name was Dominico, looked down at his friend. "When he drinks too much, he picks fights with people."

"Not anymore," intoned the proprietor.

"The gringo was very fast, no? I wonder who he is?"

"I do not know," replied the proprietor,

"but a desperado like that — I would not give him six months to live."

Don Carlos stormed into the private rooms of Don Patricio, who had passed out cold. "Have you heard the news?" roared Don Carlos.

Don Patricio opened one eye. "What news?"

"Your idiot daughter has run off with the gringo!"

Don Patricio stared at him in alarm. "You can't be serious."

"It's true — she's disappeared, and I'm going after her. Evidently she's lost her senses. That gringo will probably kill her, if the Apaches don't get them first."

"So that's what she wanted the money for," blurted Don Patricio.

"It's probably in Braddock's pocket by now."

Don Patricio struggled to understand. "I don't believe it — not my little Doña Consuelo."

"I'd thought she was a well-brought up girl, but evidently she has too much of *your* blood in her."

Don Patricio raised his chin two inches in the air. "What is *that* supposed to mean?"

Don Carlos realized that he'd insulted his old friend. He placed his hand on Don Patricio's shoulder and said, "I apologize, but I'm so angry, I'm almost beside myself."

"It does not sound like my daughter," replied Don Patricio. "She must have forgotten everything that Holy Mother Church has taught her. How could she do such a thing?"

Duane pulled back Midnight's reins, and the horse slowed on a *playa* covered with grama grass, palmilla, piñon, and scrub oak. Consuelo came to a halt beside him, sweaty and covered with alkali, her complexion blotched with exertion.

"Still with me?" Duane asked.

"You won't get rid of me that easily, señor. Perhaps my mind is playing tricks, but did you actually shoot that man back there?"

Duane couldn't help smiling, despite their grim situation. "The vaquero was drunk, and he drew first. I hope you'll remember that at the trial."

"You were so fast — I never saw you reach for your gun."

Duane leaned toward her, squeezed her shoulder, and winked. "That's why they

248

call me the Pecos Kid."

Don Carlos pounded on the door of the hut, and it was opened by Conchita, eyes wide with fear, her little son hugging her leg. The peasant woman couldn't think of anything to say as Don Carlos marched stalwartly into her parlor. "I understand that Doña Consuelo visited you yesterday around sundown, and then she left with the gringo."

"I do not know," Conchita replied unsteadily, avoiding his stare.

"You are not so dumb as you look, so you had better tell the truth. What did she say?"

"I do not remember, Don Carlos."

"Oh, yes you do." He grabbed her arm, yanked his American-made Whitney Navy revolver, and aimed between her eyes. "I'm not going to ask again."

"Please sir . . . have mercy."

"Did she mention me?"

Conchita stared down the barrel of the gun. "No sir — she gave me some money for Pepito, kissed him, and said something about destiny. Then she walked out the back door, and I have not seen her since."

"Did she act . . . ?" Don Carlos tapped his head.

Conchita sobbed. "I do not know, but I will give the money back, Don Carlos."

"What the hell do I care about your money, woman! Destiny, eh? Evidently my dear wife thinks she's in an opera by Verdi, but I shall bring her back to her senses!"

The vaquero army stood at attention as Don Carlos strolled back to the hacienda. They had bedrolls, two wagons, tents, a chuckwagon, and enough ammunition to fight a war, not to mention two crates of dynamite. Don Carlos approached García, and said: "Where is the Indian?"

"He is a half-breed." García motioned with his head, and the nobleman saw a slight man dressed like a vaquero, but his complexion was dark and he had a nose like a buzzard. "Come here," said Don Carlos.

The half-breed stepped forward, his face betraying no emotion, as if carved out of basalt.

"What is your name?"

"They call me Lázaro, sir."

"Apache?"

The Indian nodded in assent.

Don Carlos looked into his eyes. "If you locate my wife, I will make you rich for the rest of your life."

"I have already found their trail." Lázaro

pointed to the desert behind Conchita's house. "There."

Don Carlos turned to García. "Tell the men to mount up."

García passed along the order as Don Carlos climbed onto his palomino stallion. He swung the beast toward the main gate of the hacienda, and rode to the head of the long column, where he joined García and Lázaro. Don Carlos turned in the saddle and examined his tough, desert-hardened vaqueros, men accustomed to living in the open, who loved to fight, and who accepted the law of Don Carlos. The nobleman raised his hand in the air. "Forward!" he commanded.

Equipment clattered and horses' hooves thudded against the ground, as the searchers passed through the main gate. Don Carlos sat in the saddle, his eyes narrow with rage. Never had he been so humiliated, or felt like such a buffoon. He wanted to loathe Duane Braddock, but how could any normal male resist a ripe peach like Doña Consuelo? And neither could he blame her, because why shouldn't she have a young virile man for a change?

Don Carlos's anger turned inward, and he acknowledged that it was absurd to marry a woman young enough to be his daughter. Such bizarre acts are bound to bring dishonor to families, he realized.

The half-breed pointed straight ahead. "That is their trail, sir."

Don Carlos couldn't see anything, but his eyes weren't so good anymore. A doctor had told him to wear spectacles, but Don Carlos didn't like how they looked. "Proceed," he ordered.

Lázaro steered his horse onto the day-old trail, and the vaquero army fell in behind. Don Carlos placed one fist on his hip and gazed regally at vast desert wastes dotted with clumps of grazing cattle. It might take a few days, he estimated, but I will find her if it is the last thing I do. If I know my little Doña Consuelo, I'm sure that she's having doubts about the whole dubious enterprise by now, and she'll probably be delighted to see me.

Duane and Doña Consuelo stopped for a meal amid a pile of jagged boulders approximately ten feet tall, with Benson and Weniger cactus in the vicinity, plus plenty of grama grass. Duane hobbled the horses, as Doña Consuelo unpacked the food.

She sat on a flat section of ground, cross-legged like an Indian, her voluminous skirt covering knees and ankles. Her hat was low over her eyes, protecting her from the bright glare, and she was covered with a thin film of alkali dust, as insects buzzed her ears.

Doña Consuelo felt as though she were starving to death, and wanted to dig her fangs into the food, but etiquette required that she wait for her dining companion. He was scouting the campsite, carrying his rifle, behaving more like a furtive desert creature than a man. She'd seen only one facet of Duane Braddock at the hacienda, and realized now that she hadn't understood him at all. The shootout in the store had altered her evaluation drastically.

She'd known that he was brave, but it's one thing to stop a team of runaway horses, and another to shoot somebody at point-blank range. A more prudent man might've kept his mouth shut, but not Duane Braddock. Doña Consuelo couldn't banish the killing from her mind. The most discomforting part was she'd felt a strange thrill when the bullet struck the vaquero. It troubled her to acknowledge that if the fight had gone the other way, she'd be the drunken vaquero's prize.

Duane kneeled opposite her, looked around one last time, and lay his rifle on the ground. He was tense, alert, a desert cat rather than a man. He drew his knife, wiped the blade on his pants, and sliced off a chunk of meat.

"Go ahead," he said.

She took the slice, held it in her dainty fingers, and bit off the end. A stack of cold dry tortillas sat in front of them, with a canteen of water. That was the meal, but Doña Consuelo wasn't complaining. She ate ravenously, as Duane admired her lips, the swell of her breast, her natural grace.

"How're you holding up?" he asked.

"I'm all right," she replied. "What about you?"

"Couldn't be better. You're not having second thoughts?"

"Why do you keep asking that stupid question?"

"I thought you might see us in a different light after a few hours on the desert."

"I do see you in a different light, and can't help wondering why you didn't simply ignore that drunken pig in the town."

"If I ignored him, he would've insulted me again."

"What if he shot first?"

"He didn't."

"Perhaps in the future you should let *me* do the talking."

"It's all right with me. I don't claim to be an expert with drunkards."

He gnawed a fistful of beef, as his eyes scanned their surroundings. He was covered with dust, stubble showed on his chin, and he looked more outlaw than ever. A yellow bird flew overhead, examining them curiously, and then suddenly Duane was on his feet, whipping out his Colt .44.

A *jabalina* pig walked nonchalantly across the far end of the clearing, paying no attention to Duane and Doña Consuelo. The fugitives resumed their meal, and no longer did Doña Consuelo ask what she was doing with him. They finished the meal, and he repacked their saddlebags. "Let's get rolling," he told her.

"I thought we could rest awhile."

"That's what we just did."

"Not even a few more minutes?"

He pointed his finger at her nose. "Discipline is the key to survival on the desert. Now get on your horse."

"I thought we slept during the day, and rode during the night."

"Not after what happened in the store." He turned down a corner of his mouth. "Let's understand something, Doña

Consuelo. We don't have discussions about what to do, because *I'm* in charge." He slapped her on the rear end. "Now get on your horse."

Don Carlos and his vaqueros rode down the main street of a small settlement, the odor of woodsmoke heavy in the air. The trail of Duane Braddock and Doña Consuelo had led them here, and Don Carlos wondered if the culprits still were in town.

Vaqueros patrolled both sides of the street, searching for Midnight and Josephina among horses tied at the rails. Don Carlos angled his mount toward the store, as a crowd gathered to see the arrival of the great caudillo. "It is Don Carlos de Rebozo!" called one of them.

The Don was a local celebrity, and everybody wanted to say to grandchildren, *Once, long ago, I saw Don Carlos de Rebozo.* Like a hoary old warlord, he lowered himself to the ground. A vaquero took his reins, and the nobleman headed for the front door of the store. The proprietor stood in front of his counter, bowing slightly, awaiting orders. Don Carlos stomped toward him, looked him in the eye, and said: "I'm after two people, and I have reason to believe they were headed in this direction. One is a gringo, eighteen years old, approximately this tall —" Don Carlos held out his hand, "— and he usually wears black clothes. The other is a woman, twenty-one years old, approximately this tall, with black hair, very pretty. Have you seen them?"

The proprietor nodded. "They were here this morning, and the gringo shot a man right over there." He pointed at a stain on the floor. "A vaquero insulted the woman, and the gringo killed him."

Don Carlos lost his regal composure, but only for a moment. "The woman — did she appear unharmed?"

"It was clear that she and the gringo had been riding for a long distance."

"How did she act? Was she a little loco, would you say?"

"She was surprisingly calm, sir, in view of what had happened."

"Which way did they go?"

The proprietor pointed. Don Carlos walked out the door, and found the half-breed in front of the store. "They went that way," said Don Carlos, pointing ahead down the trail. "Move it out."

Lázaro headed for his horse as the caudillo faced García. "Order the men to mount up."

"Sir, the men had hoped you would let them have a glass of mescal for the trail."

"We don't have time for a party, García. I said order the men to mount up."

Don Carlos backed his horse into the dusty trail, then climbed into the saddle. He readjusted his hat, then straightened his backbone, took the reins, and looked like an old gray-mustachioed general as he led his men out of town.

Beneath his solid military demeanor, Don Carlos was deeply disturbed. Duane Braddock had claimed another victim, but the bloody news didn't fit with the naive and shy youth with whom Don Carlos had dined at the hacienda. Now that Don Carlos thought it over, Duane Braddock reminded him of students he'd known in Seville, the ones who'd spent their time in libraries, not ladies' boudoirs.

I've caused suffering to other husbands too, realized Don Carlos, and now it's coming back to me. But if I tell her how much I love her, and remind her about all she's given up, I'm certain that she'll take the prudent course.

Don Carlos thought he understood Doña Consuelo, and surmised that she was petrified with terror. Despite her recent conversion to reality, she's still fundamentally a very sheltered child, he told himself. Maybe she's ready to leave her new paramour, but is afraid he might fly into one of his rages and kill her.

Don Carlos worried about his little wife as he followed the Apache half-breed onto the desert. García caught up with Don Carlos, slowed his mount, and rode silently at the side of the nobleman, as his first sergeant. The column of twos advanced onto the open desert, hauling wagons at the rear, sending up a cloud of dust.

Don Carlos turned toward García and asked: "What do you think about all this?"

García appeared disturbed by the question. "I have no right, sir . . ."

"Forget for a moment that I'm Don Carlos and you're García. I'm asking you man to man. You've been working for me a long time, and you know me very well. Do you think I'm a fool for chasing my wife this way?"

García shrugged, and said reluctantly: "I would do the same thing, sir." The foreman of vaqueros held his forefinger to his own throat, and made a sudden motion. "The gringo has got to die. It is a matter of honor."

Of course, reflected Don Carlos. The vaqueros don't think I'm a buffoon, but a man of honor. You don't let a man run off with your wife, and even a vaquero can understand the insult. Duane Braddock has violated me in the worst possible way, and I don't care how shy and scholarly he is.

The sun sank toward vermilion mountains in the distance as Don Carlos turned toward his foreman once more. "I'm curious about something else, García. You're a married man, and you must know something about women. What would make a good religious girl like Doña Consuelo do such a thing?"

García shrugged, as if the answer were too obvious to discuss. "I grew up the only son among four sisters. My grandmother and one of my unmarried aunts also lived with us in a two room *jacal.* I have been with women all my life, and I have tried to understand them, but what man has ever understood women? They do not even understand themselves, and they are liable to do any crazy thing that comes to their minds. You can beat them, but it does no good. You can lock them up, but who has the heart to lock up a woman? How can you ask me how to handle your wife, when I cannot even handle mine?"

Don Carlos saw the absurdity of his predicament and burst into laughter. García chuckled as well. Side by side they rode onward, as the sun cast long shadows onto the desert. I'm not the first man with horns on my head, realized Don Carlos. The vaqueros understand, because what man has never been betrayed by a woman? Duane Braddock sat at table with me, pretended to be my friend, and swore that he had no designs on my wife. He has broken the silent pact that all decent men make with each other, and ignorance is no excuse. Duane Braddock must be punished for his sins.

Doña Consuelo sat in a shallow ditch, gun in hand, waiting for Duane to return. He was hunting a suitable place to spend the night, and they'd landed in a terrain of cliffs, pinnacles, buttes, and ledges, with plenty of nooks and crannies for two people to disappear inside.

Since infancy, Doña Consuelo had heard about Apaches burning, looting, slaughtering, and raping. She was prepared to blow her brains out, her pistol cocked and ready to fire, if any Apache tried to capture her. Duane had been gone a long time, or so she thought. It was a new world, and she hoped she'd be able to hold up.

"It's me," said a voice behind her. "Don't shoot."

She spun around, and he lay on the grama grass a few feet behind her, a grin on his face. "I've found a nice little cave a little farther along. Let's go."

He gathered the horses' reins and led them into a notch between two jagged escarpments. Doña Consuelo followed, as sharp stones stabbed and twisted her boots. She was utterly filthy, and wished she could take a bath, but she'd left her bathtub far behind. It's not *that* bad, she tried to convince herself, as Duane led her to the front of a cave.

"It's a perfect spot," he told her proudly. "If anybody tries to get us, they'll have to come through that passageway, and I believe they'll find it too high a price to pay. I'll take care of the horses — make yourself comfortable — be right back."

She lowered her head and entered the cave. To her surprise, the ceiling swept up after the first few feet. She raised herself to full height and saw a roundish chamber with a flat rock floor and the bones of a *lobo* in the corner. She kicked the offending ossified calcium formations out the door, then searched for a spot for the bedroll. She located a flat stretch, knelt, and unrolled the blankets where they could look out the door when they awakened. A smile came to her face as she accomplished this tender task.

He returned to the cave, took one look, and pointed to another spot. "Put the bedroll over there."

"But I like it here."

"Somebody could shoot you in bed from that passageway. Move it." He walked around the cave, kicked the wall, picked up something from the floor, and held it to his eye. "An old arrowhead. I guess we're not the first ones to sleep here."

"I hope it's not a place where Apaches come regularly."

"Nobody's been here for a long time," said Duane.

"How do you know?"

"If people visit a place, they keep the dust from settling on the floor." He bent over, scraped his finger along the rock, and held up the alkali powder. "See?"

He took off his hat, slapped it against his knee, and put it back on. Then he laid out his weapons on the floor, and made sure everything was in working order. Next he crawled to the edge of the passageway and peered into the open desert.

It was becoming dark, and no Apaches,

bounty hunters, or vaqueros of Don Carlos were visible. Duane maintained a strong facade for Doña Consuelo, but had become unsettled by the shooting in the cantina. It had come so quickly, he'd barely had time to draw. No matter where he went, or what he did, somebody started up with him. Do I carry the mark of Cain? he wondered.

Sometimes he thought he was doomed, and should go back to the monastery, but not with a beautiful woman only twenty paces away. He returned to the cave, and she was sitting on the blankets, pulling off her boots, her skirt lifting to show a length of leg. This is worth dying for, he admitted, as he moved toward her.

"Duane," she protested weakly.

He lowered her to the blankets, crawled on top, roved his hands over her hips, and kissed her lightly. "I've been dreaming about this moment all day long," he whispered. "I saw you sitting in the saddle, and I thought, *I've got to have some of that.*"

He kissed her throat, and she dug her fingernails into his thick shaggy hair. The scratch of his beard thrilled her as he unbuttoned her blouse. His hand slipped inside, and came to rest on an extremely sensitive portion of her anatomy.

"I also was looking at you today," she replied. "You sat in your saddle like a *real* caudillo, and I thought, *I can't wait until it's time to go to bed.*"

They undressed each other frantically, kissing portions of each other's emerging anatomy, tossing garments wildly through the air. Duane's heart filled with mad animal lust as he inserted his tongue into her petulant mouth. Her body undulated rhythmically beneath him, provoking his ardor to higher summits, as night came to the Apache homeland.

Frowning, Don Carlos stood at his camp table, studying a map. He and his men hadn't covered as much ground as he'd anticipated, because the fugitives's trail had petered out three hours ago on a long stretch of rock. Now the half-breed was scouting about, trying to find where they'd gone.

Don Carlos wondered whether to throw away the wagons and travel lighter. We'll never catch them at the rate we're going, and I wonder if there's a better way. Where are they headed, and can we cut them off?

Don Carlos didn't think the gringo would visit another Mexican town, after the last murder. He'd also stay off main trails, sleep where no one could find him, and live off the land, like an Indian. But he could not hide for the rest of his life, and one day I will catch him.

"Sir?" asked Lázaro, outside the tent.

"Come in."

The half-breed entered, and appeared more vital since he'd returned to the desert. "I have been unable to find his trail, sir, but in the morning I will try again."

"I'm surprised that it's taking so long," said Don Carlos. "I thought that Apaches were the best trackers in the world."

"He covers his trail well, and they say that he is part Apache too. But I know where he's headed." Lázaro smiled, showing tobacco-stained teeth. "The Sierra Madre mountains."

"Tell me the truth, half-breed. What are our real chances of finding them?"

"He does not have time to cover everything. Between here and the Sierra Madre, I will find his sign."

"What if he's gone elsewhere?"

"An Apache will hide in the Sierra Madre mountains, because no Mexicans will go there. But I was raised in those mountains, and know them well. You've heard the old saying, Don Carlos: *It takes an Apache to catch an Apache.*"

The lovers lay in each other's arms, safe from enemies, covered with a gray wool blanket, cheeks touching. "Are you awake, Duane?" she asked.

"Yes," he said softly, letting her womanly warmth thaw the knotted rage in his soul.

"I was thinking about something, and I hope you won't laugh, but — have you had many girls?"

"A few."

"A good-looking boy like you, you can probably get any one you want, no?"

"I'm not as experienced as you might think."

"I've only made love with Don Carlos, but you're so different."

Duane looked away uneasily. "I feel as if I've ruined your life, Doña Consuelo. I did everything I could to get you, and once I even tried to make you drunk on mescal."

"I wanted you to get me from the first moment I saw you," she told him. "And you will never be alone again, as long as I'm alive."

Don Carlos fretted on his canvas cot, because he knew precisely what was happening at that moment. The young lovers were alone, with the jealous husband far away, and Don Carlos tasted acids rising in his throat. He knew the story too well, because he also had tasted the heady bouquet of illicit love, as well as the ambrosia of marital bliss. He knew the mating game through all its permutations, and considered his twenties the finest time of his life.

But his twenties were over, while Doña Consuelo was at the beginning of hers. He imagined her engaged in carnal delight, while he scratched and twitched alone on his cot. He knew the commitment that she brought to love, the tiny sounds that escaped her lips, and the exquisite contortions of her body.

Don Carlos felt old, paunchy, balding, and no longer in robust health by any means. He knew that young lovers could satisfy physical appetites for hours and even days on end, with only an occasional meal and drink of water, because that was his own experience during his career as a Casanova.

His very sophistication in love was an additional source of misery, because he understood well the language of seduction. He felt imprisoned inside his canvas tent, so he rolled out of bed, pulled on his boots, strapped on his Whitney, and donned his black leather riding jacket. Then he made his way to the embers of the fire, passing vaqueros sleeping on the ground all around him. He looked at the three-quarter waxing moon poised in a sky drenched with stars. The identical moon shone on Doña Consuelo in another man's arms, and Don Carlos nearly doubled over with pain.

He couldn't stop thinking about Doña Consuelo with her shapely legs wrapped around Duane Braddock, and decided to blow his brains out. He reached for the Whitney, thumbed back the hammer, held the barrel to his right temple, and touched his finger to the trigger.

He imagined them kissing and clutching deliriously, while she'd performed the same sinful acts upon Braddock that he, Don Carlos, had taught her. His finger tightened around the trigger, and then, in a flash of logic, he saw the ramifications.

They'd say the old fool killed himself because his wife had run off with a younger man. His suffering would provide comic relief for vaqueros drunk out of their minds in cantinas, and the caudillo didn't want to be remembered that way.

He removed his finger from the trigger, eased the hammer forward, and dropped the Whitney into its holster. Be a man, not a fool, he advised himself. My ancestor was a *conquistador,* and I must set an example for those who look up to me.

Don Carlos would have preferred to fall on his knees and cry like a baby, but that was unacceptable for a caudillo. He had to find his wife, to make sure that she hadn't been kidnapped, and he had to shoot Duane Braddock.

Don Carlos hoped that his wife had gone mad, rather than having fallen for another man. I should have locked her in a closet, he said to himself, but he could never be cruel to Doña Consuelo, despite his outbursts. I must do what's expected of me, he vowed. Whatever happens, I cannot disgrace my name.

CHAPTER 9

Doña Consuelo peered out the front entrance of the cave, the ornate Colt in her right hand. It was another sunny day, the desert shone like gold, and a condor flew over the mountain pass.

Doña Consuelo felt at one with herself and the world, not missing her bathtub in the least. Duane had found a stream not far away, and she took a bath every day, washed their clothing, and sunned herself naked on the rocks, with Duane often joining her.

Their diet consisted of fresh roast meat supplemented with a variety of roots and nuts. After three weeks on the dodge, she felt like part of the desert, instead of sweet little Doña Consuelo, too refined to perform useful tasks. She wouldn't object to living in the rough forever, because at last she was getting what she needed.

But there was one major drawback: the Apaches. Because of them, she and Duane lived in constant fear of getting massacred. She pulled her head back into the cave and sat with her back to the wall.

She wished Duane could take her on jaunts, but she didn't know how to move quietly, and Apaches might hear her. She'd never dreamed that she could be so happy, but sometimes felt uneasy, and occasionally was nauseous. Can I be pregnant? she sometimes asked herself.

Duane scrambled across crags and ridges like a mountain goat, as he familiarized himself with the terrain around the cave. There were deep sudden gorges, high cliffs, and narrow passageways, not to mention small caves with animal turds on the floor. He could find no sign indicating that Apaches had been in the vicinity recently, and hoped it stayed that way.

He stopped at regular intervals, to look and listen for Apaches, and then spotted a cave a quarter of the way up a mountain to his left. It appeared that he could reach it over a steep incline strewn with boulders. He climbed the approach, drew closer, and heard a growl from within. "Sorry," he said, backing away. "Didn't mean to disturb you."

It sounded like a bear, and the Pecos Kid promptly descended the side of the promontory, because not even a .44 slug could penetrate a bear's hide. Duane came to a patch of wild lavender and soapweed on the way down, and was surprised to see a low passageway in its shadow. The opening wouldn't be visible unless someone stood a few steps away.

Duane stuck his head inside, and noted that the passageway inclined upward, leading to what looked like another small-mouthed cave. Duane crept closer, wondering if the cousin of the other bear lived there. He raised his head, but was greeted by no hostile sounds.

He peered into the cave, and it didn't look like more than crawl space. He got down on his hands and knees, inched inside, and hoped that the mountain wouldn't collapse on top of him. The space enlarged, showing a chamber larger than the one in which he currently resided. Duane found the usual pellets of animal excrement, and a dark hazy mass at the rear. Yanking his gun, advancing closer, he saw that it was another passageway. He edged himself into its dark convoluted turns, and said to himself, wait a minute — there's liable to be a mountain lion at the end of this thing.

He lit a match, and it was dark rock all around him. He felt a mild stab of panic, as if walls were crushing him to death, and decided to get the hell out of there. But I wonder where it leads? he asked himself. The narrow alley continued, and he'd heard legends about a mountain of gold somewhere in the Sierra Madre. Maybe it's straight ahead, Duane postulated. If any lion messes with me, I'll shoot his lights out.

With the Colt in his right hand, he crawled into the darkness, pausing every few lengths to look around. Then he noticed a faint glimmer coming from the other end. Have I come all the way through the mountain? wondered Duane.

He crawled toward the light, the passage widened, and he saw the opening straight ahead. Arising in a vast domed vault, it reminded him of a cathedral, with another crack at its far end. He got down on his belly, inched forward, and his eyes widened at an incredible sight.

About two hundred yards away, a deserted crumbling pueblo settlement nestled against the side of the next peak. Some sections leaned in odd angles, while others had collapsed totally. Duane wondered where the Indians had gone, as he moved down rock steps leading to the ground. The pueblo was at the edge of approximately twenty acres of grama grass, inside a cluster of mountains, the perfect hiding place.

He advanced toward the pueblo, and had an eerie feeling that Olmec and Toltec gods were watching him. He examined crags and precipices for Apaches, because the silence was peculiar, like a special little hidden world.

He entered the pueblo, and found a rectangular room with a firepit in the corner, and strange objects scattered on the floor: clay urns, the stonecarved head and headdress of a warrior, and a ceramic baby with slanted eyes and fat lips. The walls were covered with drawings that looked like warriors, maidens, and high priests. Duane didn't know what to make of it. He explored several more rooms, finding additional statues and figurines. Dropping to one knee, he picked up a clay vessel in the shape of a frog.

Duane felt dazzled by the totally unexpected appearance of another world.

Where did they go? he wondered. And why? He estimated that the artifacts came from ancient epochs of Mexico, and wondered if he were the first person to see the lost pueblo since the days before the Conquistadores.

He snooped about for signs of intruders, but nothing human had been there for years. He located a natural spring not far from the pueblo, and it filled a pond where Consuelo could bathe.

It's our paradise, and nobody else will ever stumble onto it, because it's so damned hard to find. Hell, we could spend the rest of our lives here, and even raise a family.

Don Carlos sat in his tent, smoking his last cigarillo. He wore a gray beard, his eyes were black coals, and his paunch was rapidly disappearing. He and his vaqueros had been wandering the desert nearly a month, as Lázaro lost and found Braddock's trail repeatedly. It was slow painstaking progress, and Don Carlos wondered if he should go home. Surely a month of intensive search was sufficient to wipe out any stain on the Rebozo family escutcheon.

But Don Carlos still missed Doña

Consuelo, and couldn't give up the chase yet. She might be behind the next mesa, or in the next town, he said to himself. Perhaps she'll realize that Duane Braddock is just a boy, whereas I am the fellow for whom she's really yearning.

Don't deceive yourself, said a little voice in the corner of his ear. You may cut a fine figure of a man, but you're just an old fogy to her. Yet hope burned faintly in the nobleman's breast, despite common sense and all indications to the contrary.

The tent flap was thrown aside, and García stuck his head inside. "The half-breed is back."

Don Carlos put on his hat and stepped into the cool January afternoon. They were camped on the usual cactus-strewn plateau with mountains in the distance, but the vistas of Mexico never failed to fascinate Don Carlos. The half-breed rode toward him, sitting erect in his saddle, and Don Carlos couldn't help admiring him, because Lázaro seemed to thrive on the desert.

Lázaro stopped his horse in front of Don Carlos, then descended from the saddle, and bowed slightly. "I have picked up their trail," he said. "They have gone into the Sierra Madre mountains, and I have a good idea where. I think that we should move closer, but not too close. Then I will examine the area myself, while the rest of you wait nearby. Sooner or later I will see them. They cannot hide forever."

"How long?" asked Don Carlos.

"I might find them in a day, or it might be six months."

"Six months!" exploded Don Carlos.

Lázaro spoke no words, but his silence seemed to be saying: *she's your wife — not mine.*

Don Carlos could feel the eyes of the vaqueros upon him, and their fierce pride demanded vengeance. I can't give up now, he thought, especially since Lázaro has found their trail. "García — direct the men to prepare for departure first thing in the morning. Lázaro will tell you the direction of our march."

It was Saturday night at the new enlarged Last Chance Saloon, and Maggie O'Day puffed a cigar as she walked down the corridor to Vanessa's room. She knocked on the door — no answer, so she turned the knob.

Miss Vanessa Fontaine sat on her upholstered chair, sniffling into a handkerchief. Her cosmetics were smeared, and the last show would begin in five minutes.

"Are you sick?" asked Maggie O'Day.

"Leave me alone," replied Escondido's foremost entertainer.

"But it's time to go to work!"

Vanessa shook her head, and made a soft sobbing sound.

"What's wrong?" asked Maggie, becoming alarmed.

"I don't feel well."

"You'll have plenty of time to sleep after the show."

"I can't go on."

Maggie placed the back of her hand against Vanessa's forehead, but the Charleston Nightingale didn't have a fever. "Is there pain?"

Vanessa sighed. "He'll never show up, and I'm wasting my time."

Now Maggie understood the nature of the illness. "I ain't a-gonna argue with you, but you've got a roomful of mean sons-of-bitches out thar, and some of 'em's come a long way to see you. If you don't sing at least one song, they'll tear this goddamned place apart, and besides, Duane said he'd stop when he comes over the border. I'm sure he'll keep his word."

"What if he's dead, or in some Mexican jail?"

"I wouldn't bet on anybody killing the Pecos Kid, and the lawman hasn't been born who could take him into custody. Yes, maybe this'll be the night he walks through that door. You'd better get out there and see, otherwise there might not be a Last Chance Saloon come tomorrow morning."

A few blocks away, ex-sheriff J. T. Sturgis sat in his dingy room and counted forty dollars in coins. My money is running out, and maybe it's time I gave up this wild goose chase.

Sturgis felt disgusted with himself, because he'd invested heavily in the enterprise. Why'd I shoot off my big mouth about how I was a-gonna arrest Duane Braddock? I should've kept quiet, collected my salary, and nailed his ass to the door when he showed up in town.

I'd better find a cowboy job afore I git completely played out, he figured, but workin' cattle is the dumbest job in the world. And for all I know, Duane Braddock might show up tomorrow night. Maybe I'll give it another two weeks, and then look fer a job. I've put a lot into this already — be foolish not to see it through.

He strapped on his Remington, then tied the holster to his leg. Maybe this'll be my big night, he thought, as he looked at himself in the mirror.

The lamplight showed a corporal in the Confederate Army, wearing his gray uniform and kept with crossed gold rifles. He smiled ruefully, as he thought about what might've been. If we'd only captured Cemetery Ridge, he mused.

He remembered the precise moment that the attack had failed. It was in the vortex of Bloody Angle, where Americans in blue, gray, and butternut fought hand to hand and man to man with bayonets, rifle butts, and anything else they could lay their hands on. It had been down and dirty, the ground had run red with blood, and heaps of bodies had been everywhere.

Sturgis's face glowed with shame as he saw himself take that first step backwards, but the 9th Virginia had been flayed by fire from three directions, while Yankee reinforcements had poured into the gap. Corporal Sturgis had run helter-skelter toward his lines, had barely eluded death on countless occasions, and, like many exhausted and demoralized survivors of Pickett's famous charge, had ended in front of General Lee's command post.

The great man in his gray beard and gray uniform had appeared dumbfounded, as he walked among the returning soldiers, trying to comfort them. Sturgis had stumbled toward him, bowed his head, and felt like crying.

And then he had heard General Lee's voice. "I'm sorry. It was my fault. Forgive me."

J. T. Sturgis would never forget that moment. The old Grey Fox had been broken by the slaughter he'd ordered with his own mouth, but he didn't blame it on anybody else, as some officers might've done. Sturgis had collapsed shortly afterwards, and awakened in the medical tent with his leg sewn up, but at least he was alive, and privileged to have seen true nobility before his eyes for once in his failed life.

He knew that the War of Northern Aggression had ended nearly seven years ago, and since had become the bailiwick of historians. Some told the story from one point of view, and others told it from another, while every general was anxious to protect his reputation, and each enlisted man wanted to believe that he'd been engaged in a great historic enterprise. But J. T. Sturgis knew that whatever happened in history books, he'd seen brilliance in the person of General Lee. It had nothing to do with winning or losing battles, but was about being a man of honor.

General Lee had been a fighter, he didn't make excuses, and J.T. loved him for it. The ex-corporal looked at the hand that had shaken the hand of Robert E. Lee, and his fingers tingled with pride. The finest gentleman in the South didn't give up after Pickett's Charge, and neither will I, Sturgis told himself. I'm going to see this damned Braddock thing through to the bitter end.

Duane sat in front of the pueblo, looking at the swirling heavens. "I wonder if there are any cowboys out there?" he mused.

Doña Consuelo reclined next to him, in her worn suede jacket and skirt. "I wonder what happened to the people who lived here?"

"Maybe their enemies found them, and they went on the dodge. But your guess is as good as mine. At any rate, we can hide forever, if we want."

He touched her shoulder, and she never resisted. Their lips brushed as his palms came to rest on her waist. Gradually they sank toward the ground, fumbling with each other's buttons. He touched his lips to her nipple, and had the odd feeling that they were making love on a former altar of the Toltec religion.

"I love this place," she whispered. "I don't think I've ever been so happy."

"Me neither," he replied, as he removed her blouse. They rolled across the altar, biting and scratching like puppies, as ghosts of ancient gods with earrings looked down at them, and a comet shot across the Milky Way.

CHAPTER 10

Lázaro lay on his belly, observing the foothills of the Sierra Madre mountains. Every day he selected a new hiding spot, waited patiently, and scanned. His sharp eyes had noticed remnants of boot tracks the previous afternoon, and that very morning he'd heard a distant shot. Sooner or later he'll have to show himself, figured Lázaro.

Duane Braddock had come in this direction, but erased his trail before entering the foothills. Oh *Yusn*, please send him to me, prayed Lázaro. I want to be rich for a change.

He was afraid the hunt would be called off soon, because Don Carlos didn't appreciate the importance of time, or maybe he didn't really love his wife, and that's why she'd left him. In the Apache religion, a man had the right to cut off his wife's nose, if he found her with another man.

Lázaro noticed movement in the corner of his eye. Someone or something was passing through desert foliage, headed toward the foothills. It could be a mule, deer, coyote, *jabalina* pig, or maybe the Pecos Kid. Lázaro focused his eyes toward branches scraping back and forth across the ground.

It sounded like a man covering his tracks, and Lázaro gave thanks to *Yusn*, the mountain spirits, and White Painted Woman. He raised his rifle and lined up the sights. The gringo emerged in an open stretch between scraggly cottonwood trees. Branches in hand, he worked over his backtracks. Visions of wealth flooded Lázaro's mind — he could buy another wife, a few more horses, a big house, and all the mescal he ever wanted.

His finger tightened around the trigger, but then he remembered Doña Consuelo. She was the prize, not the gringo. Lázaro waited until his quarry was out of the sight, then ran forward, pressed his back to a rock wall, peered around the corner, and saw the gringo running up the side of a pass, lithe as an Apache.

Lázaro waited cautiously, to make sure

the gringo wasn't coming back, then advanced swiftly and silently through the underbrush, heading toward the spot where the gringo had disappeared. Lázaro arrived in time to see the gringo crawling into a cave. The half-breed smiled happily as he crouched behind a scattering of artemisia and aloe bushes. I knew I'd find you someday, Mister Pecos Kid.

Doña Consuelo had finished her daily bath, her black hair wet and glistening in the sunlight, and was dressing as Duane approached. "I've been thinking," he said. "Maybe it's time we were moving on."

"To where?" she asked.

"Back to Texas."

They returned to the pueblo, her heart sinking with every step. She knew about Duane's father and mother, how they'd been killed in a range war, and why the Pecos Kid must avenge their deaths. Paradise was coming to an end, and she hadn't yet told him of her pregnancy, for fear it might undermine their idyllic existence.

"When are we leaving?" she asked.

"A few more days. We'll cross the border near Escondido, where I've got friends." His eyes roved her downturned features.

"You don't look too happy about it."

"I am afraid of what is going to happen."

"Nothing will happen if we stay alert, and keep our guns ready to fire."

Don Carlos slept on his cot, dreaming of castles and cathedrals in Old Seville. He'd had jet black hair in those days, and moved about the best drawing rooms with all the mock confidence and silly goals of youth. He'd wanted to change the world, and had thought he was destined for a greatness that continued to elude him, for he knew, deep in his heart, that compared to a man like Benito Juárez, President of Mexico, Don Carlos de Rebozo was just a big frog in a small pond.

"Don Carlos," said a voice near his ear.

He opened his eyes. Seville disappeared, and he was an old man sleeping in a breezy tent. "Who's there?" he asked fearfully, because he thought perhaps Death had come for him.

"It is Lázaro, sir, and I have good news. I have found them."

Don Carlos came to his senses instantly. "Are you sure?"

"I saw the gringo and the cave where he went."

"What about my wife?"

"She is in the cave with him, I think."

Maybe the gringo has killed her, conjectured Don Carlos. Or perhaps he's tied and bound her so that she can't leave him. The nobleman rolled out of bed, craved a cigarillo, but they were long gone. He lit the lamp, as Lázaro stood near the front flap of the tent, his features showing no emotion. Don Carlos pulled on his pants and thumbed his suspenders over his shoulders. "Get me García," he said. "We're moving out at once."

The first ray of dawn peeked through the window of the pueblo as Duane opened his eyes. He rolled over and reached for Doña Consuelo, but she wasn't there. Then he heard the sound of retching outside. He grabbed his gun and saw her bent over, clutching her stomach, vomiting onto the ground. He brought her a basin of water so she could wash her face.

"It is nothing," she replied.

"You haven't been looking well, lately. Are you sure you're all right?"

She made her sad smile, and then it hit him. "My God — you're pregnant!"

She nodded.

His jaw fell open. "Is it mine?"

She became angry for a moment, then

said: "Who else?"

"I thought maybe Don Carlos —"

"I lived with Don Carlos three years, but nothing happened. Then I slept with you, and now I'm pregnant. You are the father, I am certain. Besides, I have not done it for a long time with Don Carlos."

Don Carlos and his vaqueros sent up a thick plume of dust as they rode through the Sierre Madre mountains. The nobleman sat in his saddle, exhilarated by news that the gringo had been found. He was certain he'd see his beloved wife within the next several days.

If I know my dear Doña Consuelo, I'm sure that she misses her luxuries, not to mention her maids. I wouldn't be surprised if she were longing for me, because a woman her age needs a gentleman, not a trigger-happy child.

He tried not to worry that she was dead, or sold to the Apaches by Duane Braddock. Lázaro had said they'd reach their destination that night, if they didn't stop too long for meals and rest. The men ate tortillas in the saddle, because every moment was precious. I can't wait to gaze upon her sublime features, thought Don Carlos de Rebozo. And as for the Pecos

Kid, my vaqueros can use him for target practice.

Duane and Doña Consuelo sat in front of the fire as a loin of antelope spattered over the glowing coals. The sun sank behind the mountains, and a flight of desert bats darted over the pueblo. Duane wished he could smoke a cigarette, but was out of tobacco. A swig of mescal wouldn't hurt either, but they'd finished the bottle long ago.

He couldn't stop thinking about his unborn child. It might be a boy, and I can make him into a man, or maybe it'll be a little girl who I can spoil. He didn't know whether to remain with his woman and child, or go to the Pecos Country and avenge the murder of his parents.

He glanced at Doña Consuelo, who was tanned and toughened, with hardening muscles, minus baby fat. She looked partially a wild Indian, while the pride of her Spanish heritage shone forth brightly. He knew that he needed her, and that tipped the scales in her favor.

She turned the loin on the spit, and he admired the curve of her rear end. Her profile was nothing short of breathtaking, while the surge of her bosom filled him with renewed desire. Maybe I can track down Mister Archer after my children are grown up. He'll probably be dead by then, and I'll probably be too old to ride the vengeance trail, so it looks like the old son-of-a-bitch'll get away with the murder of my parents.

It was a big nasty lump in his craw that refused to go down. Duane examined the issue from every angle, but it added up the same. Doña Consuelo watched her man wilt before her eyes, and she knew what was bothering him. She touched his stubbled cheek with her calloused palm.

"Don't worry, *querido mío*," she said. "I do not want you to give up your life for me, and I would not respect a man who could ignore the murder of his parents. I will go with you to *Tejas*, and help you find the criminal. No one will suspect a poor pregnant Mexican woman and her vaquero husband. Then, when the stain of dishonor has been wiped out, we will start a cattle business together."

She said it matter-of-factly, like a wife discussing the family budget, but Duane felt as though a horse had been lifted off his shoulders. He straightened his spine, the corners of his mouth turned up, and they fell into each other's arms, as was their custom.

★ ★ ★

Don Carlos pushed his men all night and most of the next day. At sundown, Lázaro suggested that they make camp near a certain *arroyo*. Don Carlos passed the order down, and the men dismounted approximately two miles from Duane Braddock's hideout, close enough to strike against him on foot, but too far for Braddock to see or hear them. No fires were permitted, with no loud sounds. A vaquero unrolled Don Carlos's blankets, as the caudillo gazed at the Sierra Madre mountains looming like an incomprehensible mass of shapes and sizes in the moonlit night.

Don Carlos crossed himself, then prayed that Doña Consuelo was still alive. He was anxious for dawn, for that was when he and his men would attack the cave. He thought of her smooth belly, and how he'd brush his lips across her breasts. Worried about her safety, not to mention her virtue, he believed that any vile act was possible with a cold-blooded killer like the Pecos Kid. I'm confident that I can win her back, if she's still alive, he tried to convince himself. And if Duane Braddock killed her, justice will be administered tomorrow, so help me God.

★ ★ ★

After the last show of the evening, Miss Vanessa Fontaine often returned to the saloon for a few drinks with the boys. It was better than sitting alone in her room, moping over a certain lost outlaw, and she'd discovered that cowboys, gamblers, and thieves could be highly entertaining companions, with incredible stories to tell.

She emerged into the saloon, where a ripple of applause attended her progress. She was headed toward a round table from which a cowboy had invited her for a drink with a rancher named Spencer Reynolds and his cattle crew. As she approached, Reynolds arose with his cowboys. He was three inches shorter than she, with a sturdy chest, powerful arms, and a friendly Texas smile. A cowboy held out a chair for her, and she sat on its edge daintily. A glass of whiskey was pushed in front of her, as they ogled her with worship, lust, curiosity, and fascination.

"Here's to Miss Vanessa Fontaine!" declared the rancher.

Everyone clicked glasses, a cheer went up from the crowd, and even the saloon cat was watching from her perch atop the bar.

The rancher and the Charleston belle examined each other across the table, and

294

she could sense that he was a solid Texan, almost good-looking, clean-shaven, confident, and energetic.

"I've been in some concert halls in my time, ma'am," he said, "but you're just about the finest singer I ever heard. You put real feeling into those old songs, and for a few moments, I thought I was back in the Army."

"Where did you serve?"

"I was on the staff of General Ambrose Hill."

They exchanged pleasantries about the war, as his cowboys excused themselves one by one, then drifted toward the bar. Soon Vanessa and the rancher were alone, and he moved closer, to pour another round. His muscles strained the sleeves of his shirt, he wore no wedding ring, and she liked his roguish smile.

"I visited Charleston once, before the war," he told her. "My cousin Jimmie was a cadet at the Citadel, and I attended several parties. Perhaps we've met before."

"I'm sure that I would've remembered you, sir. What brought you to Texas?"

"The chance to start out fresh again. How about you?"

"A little dispute with the federal government known as Reconstruction."

"Why don't you come to the ranch sometime," he invited. "I'd love to have you as my guest."

I'm sure you would, she thought, as she looked him over critically. He could provide anything a former Charleston belle might require, but he evoked no powerful attraction, whereas she could become passionate by merely reflecting upon vague memories of Duane Braddock.

"Perhaps someday," she said.

"It's been this way all my life," he admitted. "The ones I like — don't like me, and vice versa."

"I'm sure you're a fine gentleman," replied Vanessa, "but what you suggest must be inspired by love, and I'm promised to someone else. You mustn't take it personally."

He laughed darkly. "Of course — how could I take it personally? You probably get twenty proposals a night."

"More," she replied, "and now, if you'll excuse me, I've got something to do."

In her dressing room, she scrutinized herself in the mirror. Every day she found new wrinkles, her hair didn't appear as thick as formerly, and her complexion appeared pallid. I'm getting older every minute, and I just threw away a perfectly good man — for what?

She flopped onto the chair, and the air went out of her lungs. Maybe I've never grown up, but if I can't trust my poor heart, what can I trust? On the other hand, I can't wait for that damned Pecos Kid forever, can I?

CHAPTER 11

Duane opened his eyes, and it was dark in the pueblo. He kissed his woman lightly on the cheek, strapped on his Colt, and tied the holster to his leg. Doña Consuelo looked like a sleeping peasant girl as the first glimmer of dawn appeared over the tops of mountains.

"Where are you going so early?" she asked sleepily.

"Lots to do."

He put on his cowboy hat and was out the door. The sun rose in the sky as he passed the altar and ascended the stepping stones to the exit from paradise. The sky brightened, as stars faded into the morning, and birds sang happily. He entered the vault, got down on his hands and knees, and made his way to the exit on the far side. As always, he approached carefully, raised his eyes over the ledge, and examined every blade of grass and cactus as far as the eye could see. The Apaches had hammered vigilance into his skull, and he repeated the ritual every time he went out.

Nothing seemed out of order, and he couldn't imagine danger in the offing. He stalked down the incline, holding his rifle in both hands, ready to fire. Suddenly, out of the peace and purity of the morning, he heard the familiar voice of Don Carlos de Rebozo: "Don't move, Braddock — or you're a dead man!"

Duane's heart stuttered — he was taken totally by surprise, and didn't know whether to collapse or go blind. Don Carlos and his vaqueros materialized out of the desert, all aiming rifles, shotguns, and pistols at him. The Pecos Kid thought he was going to faint from shock.

"Drop the rifle," said the bedraggled Don Carlos, who resembled Rip Van Winkle. "We won't hesitate to shoot."

Duane considered reaching for his Colt, but didn't have a prayer in hell. He was too far from the cave to run back, so he grinned, shrugged, and said: "Looks like you've got me." His rifle clattered to the ground.

"Now lay your revolver down . . . slowly."

Duane was afraid they'd shoot him like a dog, and he had to make a play. Fear pumped powerful chemicals into his bloodstream, and he dove to the side like an Apache, rolled over, and came up firing. Two vaqueros were hit. Then he rolled out and ran in a zig-zag toward the cave, as bullets flew like bees all around him. He was certain he'd be killed at any moment as he dived into the entrance, and a bullet pierced his left calf as his head cleared the opening.

He jolted in pain, his head hit the roof of the tunnel, and he nearly knocked himself cold. But potent glandular juices enlivened his muscles, and he squirmed into the main vault. Blood dripped into his boot, but he ran toward the rear crack and hobbled down the steps. Doña Consuelo looked out the window, an expression of panic on her face, her rifle in her hands. "What happened!" she cried.

"Your husband has arrived," replied Duane, as he hobbled across the clearing, "and he's got his whole private army with him. Get your head down." She ducked as he entered the pueblo, dropped to his stomach, and said, "Fix my leg."

She rolled up his pantleg, and saw the ugly wound. "I think that the bullet is still in there."

"Cut it out. Put your knife in the fire first, to sterilize it."

"Duane, I . . ."

"Don't worry about hurting me. I can handle the pain."

It was ferocious, and he required all his strength to keep a straight face. He didn't want to scare her, but then a terrific explosion rocked the canyon, and Doña Consuelo dived to the floor. Flying rocks struck the outer wall of the pueblo, while a few flew through the window. The sound echoed thunderously around the walls of the canyon, and Duane knew that he and his woman were in serious trouble. They looked at each other fearfully in the bright dawn light as the voice of Don Carlos came to them from the smoking mouth of the vault above. "Braddock — can you hear me!"

Duane looked at Consuelo and whispered: "He's your husband — what do you think we should do?"

"I know him very well, and maybe I can manage him." She crawled toward the open door, and shouted outside: "Don Carlos — it's me!"

There was a pause, then: "Thank heaven! Are you all right?"

"I *was* fine. What are you doing!"

"I have come to save you, my dear."

"Don't tell me that you've followed me all the way here, Don Carlos. Have you gone mad?"

"I am madly in love with you, and I want you to come back with me."

"Never! Leave me alone!"

It was silent for a few moments, and Consuelo thought she heard coughing inside the vault. Then Don Carlos replied: "I don't believe you're speaking with your own free will. For all I know, Braddock has got a gun pointed at the back of your head. Let's have a family discussion, just the both of us, where he can't influence you. Then, if you decide that you want to stay with him, it's all right with me."

"Let me think about it," she replied.

"You have five minutes."

"Only *five* minutes?"

"My dear, there's something you don't seem to understand," said Don Carlos icily. "You have disgraced my family name and yours too, you may be interested to know. But I am willing to forgive you, if you renounce the error of your ways. Otherwise, and I'm not bluffing here, I'll blow

302

that pueblo down around your ears."

There was silence for a few moments, then she replied: "You'd *kill* me?"

"Without hesitation, because you have killed something in me. It is only because I love you that I am willing to take such an extreme step."

Doña Consuelo turned to Duane. "I think he's serious."

"I've always thought there was something odd about him, but he's your husband, not mine."

"Perhaps I can talk sense to him." She moved closer to the window and cupped her hands around her mouth. "Don Carlos — we can have a family discussion in neutral territory, such as the middle of the clearing. That way I don't have to trust you too much, and you don't have to trust me."

"How do I know that Braddock won't shoot me?"

"How do I know that *you* won't shoot *me*, after what I've done to your family honor . . . ?"

"It's Braddock I don't trust."

"If he shoots you, your vaqueros will not let him leave this place alive. But if we talk, perhaps we can work out an arrangement."

There was silence for several moments, then Don Carlos said: "Very well. If Braddock kills me, my blood will be on your hands."

"Nobody wants your blood, my dear husband. The problem is that you want ours." Then she turned toward Duane. "I wish I had a mirror. How do I look?" She pinched her cheeks, bit her lips, and smoothed her hair. "I will do my best."

Duane watched her leave the pueblo, while Don Carlos warily descended the rock staircase, his rifle in his right hand, as his vaqueros sat at the edge of the vault, guns in their hands. Duane's left leg was turning numb, the bleeding had stopped, and a hunk of lead had taken up residence in his flesh. He held his knife over the fire, feeling guilty about stealing Don Carlos's wife. I'm an adulterer, I'm going to be a father, and I probably won't survive this day, thought the Pecos Kid.

Doña Consuelo walked confidently across the open ground, heading toward Don Carlos, who had come to the bottom of the stone steps. He looked like a tall Santa Claus in a wide-brimmed *estancia* hat, as he smiled gallantly. "You're looking well, and your life in the fresh air must agree with you. Shall we sit like civilized people and discuss this matter from a rational point of view?"

She dropped to a cross-legged position opposite him, astonished by how old he'd become. His gray beard made him appear grandfatherly, while his jaunty vaquero hat gave him a droll aspect. This is my husband? she asked herself. My God.

He unscrewed his canteen and passed it to her. Above them, high in the sky, three old buzzards circled hungrily, while singing insects greeted the new day. "I never thought you'd leave me, Doña Consuelo," said Don Carlos sadly. "What happened?"

"I have fallen in love with Duane Braddock. It was not my intention, and I meant you no harm. You shouldn't blame him, because he was as afraid as I."

Don Carlos examined his wife carefully, and she appeared a feral desert creature, her dignified manners vanished. "Are you happy?" he asked.

"Very," she replied.

His heart felt whacked by a meat cleaver, while his wife had become more beautiful, glowing with good health, eyes sparkling, with new grace and confidence. But what Don Carlos lacked in youth, he made up in experience, deviousness, and low cunning.

305

"You must love him very much to live like this," he said, gazing at the ruined old pueblo. "How do you get along without your maids?"

"I don't require maids," she replied, "and sleeping on the ground isn't bad once you get used to it. Of course, the diet is fairly monotonous, and there's always the danger that an Apache will cut our throats, but other than that, life couldn't be better."

"In other words, you're not coming back with me."

"I am sorry to hurt you, but I am afraid that is so, Don Carlos."

He smiled bitterly. "I guess you never loved me at all."

"You were kind to me, and we've had wonderful times together. But I have fallen in love with another man."

Don Carlos gazed at the pueblo where Duane was hiding. "What is it about him that you love?"

"Everything," she replied without hesitation.

"But is love merely physical passion? What about the spiritual side of life?"

"We have that too."

A new barb entered the nobleman's heart, because he'd believed that he and

Doña Consuelo had enjoyed a sacred inner bond. "You don't miss the old hacienda at all?"

"I must be with my man."

He reached his long bony fingers toward her face, then let his hand hang in the air. "Has he put a spell on my dear little Doña Consuelo? He's not mistreating you, is he? Has he threatened to kill you, if you don't say the right things?"

She looked him in the eye. "Don Carlos, I am aware that this is very difficult to accept, but it is not the end of the world. The Church will grant you an annulment, and you will find another young wife soon, because you are still a handsome man."

"Do you really think so?" he asked, hoping against hope that the morning sun revealed him in an attractive new light.

"Of course," she replied, because his aging narcissism had been her companion for three long years. "Wherever Don Carlos goes, women throw themselves at him. Perhaps you should make a more intelligent choice next time."

"But you were so beautiful, and you are even more beautiful now. I cannot live without you, I'm afraid."

She tried to make light of it. "Soon you'll grow accustomed to another woman, and be happier than you ever were with me."

"I do not fall in love every day," he said darkly.

"Neither do I," she replied.

"I've seen your kind before," he warned. "One day that killer of yours will throw you out, and you'll go from man to man until your self-respect is gone. Then you'll drink yourself to death in some tiny little room, impoverished, toothless, and alone."

"You say that you love me, but you do not know me at all. It would be funny were it not so tragic."

He narrowed his eyes and pinched his lips together. "There's something you don't seem to understand, my dear little Consuelo. You have disgraced me, and I'm a proud man."

"The Bible says that pride goeth before a fall, my dear husband, but it's not your fault that I'm a slut, and you should be glad to get rid of me."

"But I'm not," he replied. "I still love you in spite of myself."

"You're not the first man whose wife has left him, just as my mother wasn't the first woman betrayed by her husband. You have many good years left, but you're wasting precious time on someone who has proven unworthy of you."

He leaned toward her, raised an eyebrow, and said, "It's not going to be that easy, because I have a reputation to uphold. You may call it conceit, but I will kill Duane Braddock for what he's done. After that, you can go where you please."

The nobleman's eyes glittered with madness, and she shuddered uncontrollably. She and Duane were trapped, while the vaqueros were waiting with sticks of dynamite. "But I don't love you, Don Carlos. How can you force me to go back with you?"

"If I can't have you, neither will anybody else. And the most pathetic part is that you would tire of him after a few years. He's probably seduced men's wives before. What would you do if he left you?"

"He'd never leave me," she replied adamantly.

He smiled, as he peered into her eyes. "But my dear — you've made the same solemn vow to me before the altar of Christ, in the presence of the bishop, and look at what *you've* done. No, none of us can trust each other — how about your mother and father, for example? You possessed wealth, reputation, and family, but you gave it up for a dab of cheap romance."

"I love him," she insisted. "That's all I know."

"Come back to your husband, and all shall be forgiven. You can have your own apartment within the hacienda, and help me manage the *estancia*."

The offer was tempting, and she'd be heiress to two great fortunes soon. Don Carlos saw her weakening. "You wouldn't have to sleep with me ever, if you didn't want to," he whispered. "Just as long as you're my wife outside the bedroom."

Doña Consuelo recalled Duane lying in the cave, a bullet in his leg. Duane represented ecstasy, whereas Don Carlos was a fine gentleman of the old school. Doña Consuelo was forced to admit that she preferred the ecstasy. "I'm sorry," she said. "I can't leave him."

Her remark struck Don Carlos like a slap in the face, and Spanish anger filled his veins. "You're trying my patience," he said testily. "Are you *really* prepared to die for this vagabond killer? How'd you like to be crushed to death beneath tons of rock?"

"You must love me very much, to want to kill me."

"Correct," he replied.

She swallowed hard, and the little voice in her ear said, *Don't you think your child should have a say in the matter?* "There's something I haven't told you, Don Carlos," she began. "You may be interested to know that your heir is sleeping in my belly even as we speak."

His ears perked up. "You're pregnant?"

She nodded, and made her mysterious smile. Don Carlos felt as if the Pinta, Niña, and Santa María had fallen onto him. He gasped, coughed, and nearly choked to death, as he clutched his throat. "Are you lying to me?"

"You kill me," she replied, "you kill your son or daughter too."

"You mean Braddock's son or daughter."

"Legally I am married to you. The boy, if he is a boy, will be the son that you've always dreamed of."

Don Carlos was seldom at a loss for words, but his tongue felt welded to the roof of his mouth. He tried to peer into her uterus, to see the next of the proud Rebozos, born of the magnificent Doña Consuelo. As for the baby's father, no one had to know the truth. "Let's make a deal," said Don Carlos. "I'll let the gringo go free if you come back and have my child. I will give you my word and anything else you want, including your own hacienda."

"And after the child is born?"

"You may go wherever you want, and I'll never bother you again. If you really love the gringo, it seems a small price to pay for his life, no? And yours too, for that matter, although you don't seem to care much about it these days. I give you the word of the Rebozos, but if you choose to be stubborn, I shall proceed to destroy you and your gringo Romeo. Think it over carefully, my dear Juliet. Three lives hang in the balance here, and you can save them all."

Doña Consuelo shivered, terrified by the destructive power of love. Don Carlos had guns and dynamite, while her only resource was a boyfriend with a hole in his leg. "You're a swine to do this to me, Don Carlos. I will curse your name forever."

"And I will curse yours, so we're even."

She knit her brow in contemplation. A year without Duane would be better than seeing him dead, and the little creature within deserved a chance at life. "All right," she said grudgingly. "I have your word that you won't kill Duane Braddock?"

Don Carlos raised his right hand. "On the bones of Don Diego de Rebozo, I swear it."

"Would you let me say goodbye to him?"

"I'll give you a half hour, and I hope you won't let him talk you into dying for him."

She returned to the pueblo, her heart heavy. She didn't know how to tell Duane the truth, because he was capable of rash acts. He sat in the room, tying a rag torn from an old shirt around his calf. "I took the bullet out myself," he said, holding it up. "What did your husband have to say?"

She kneeled in front of Duane and looked into his eyes. "Listen carefully, *querido mío*, because we are in a very bad situation here. My husband is madly in love with me, unfortunately, and is willing to kill the three of us, if I don't go back to him for a year, and give him this baby."

"But it's *my* baby!" countered Duane.

"It is going to be a dead baby, unless we accede to the demands of Don Carlos. He is perfectly capable of blowing up this pueblo onto our heads. I have decided that it's better for all of us to live than die, and after a year, you and I can be together again."

"You'll never come back to me," he said in a low voice. "You'll get used to your big feather bed and your maids, and you'll forget about this poor old cowpoke who loves you so much."

A tear came to her eye. "Let's not argue

with each other, *querido mío,* because we have only a few more minutes left together. Kiss me, and don't make it worse than it is."

He clasped his arms around her, but was dizzy from pain. Together, they dropped to the blanket, and lay on their sides, her breasts pressing his chest. "I don't know how I can live without you for a year," he said.

"It's not so long. We can meet in any border town that you name."

"I'll come for you, but I'm afraid you'll change your mind."

"Never," she replied. "I'll wait for you forever, and I swear it on my baby's life."

CHAPTER 12

Doña Consuelo rocked from side to side as her horse plodded across the desert. She turned in the saddle, and gazed longingly at the jumble of crags in the distance, as sand devils rose to the sky. She imagined Duane limping painfully, saddling his horse, and preparing to leave on his mission of vengeance.

It will be a long year, she realized, and many things can happen. She recalled a passage from I Corinthians:

Love bears all things,
believes all things,
hopes all things,
endures all things.

She prayed that her man wouldn't be

killed in the final reckoning, and feared that she'd never see him again. Maybe the gringos will put him in jail, or perhaps he'll become a saint, for there still is the seminary student in him. What a strange man is the father of my child, she ruminated, as she touched her palm to her belly. Please spare his life, *Madre Mía*.

Duane couldn't stop thinking about Doña Consuelo, as if his heart were riding in her saddlebags. He saddled his horse glumly, tied on the bedroll, threw over the saddlebags, and climbed into the saddle. "Let's move it out," he said to Midnight. "We're on our way to Escondido."

Not that shithole, Midnight seemed to reply, as he worked his way down the narrow mountain path.

"Got an old friend there," explained Duane, "and I happen to know that the stable has a roof that doesn't leak."

If we make it that far.

Duane's left leg was numb, and he feared amputation. Maybe I can find a doctor, he thought hopefully. Besides, lots of men get around all right on peg legs. They'll give me whiskey, tie me down, and saw it off. But what's a leg when true love is concerned?

He felt as though an elemental portion of his being had disappeared, as every step carried her and their child farther away. In a year, that old fart will twist her head around, and I'll never see her again. When the chips are down, no woman worth her salt will ever leave her child.

Doña Consuelo lay alone in the tent, while Don Carlos slept among vaqueros near the chuckwagon. The blankets seemed cold, clammy, and dead, and she wondered how she could exist without her man. I've fallen in love, she surmised, and only God can help me now.

She placed her palms on her stomach, and felt the tiny being feeding on the juices of her body. You must always be brave, act honorably, and never be afraid to love, whether you're a little boy or a little girl. Then your father and mother will be proud of you, and you will truly be our child.

Duane slouched in his saddle as Midnight carried him across a vast cactus plateau. It was two o'clock in the morning, and Duane was contemplating his lost love, when he caught a flicker of light down the road.

He halted Midnight, pulled his spyglass, and focused on a small conglomeration of buildings straight ahead. There was nothing but trouble in towns, but he worried about his leg. Maybe they've got a doctor, he thought hopefully, although the town appeared too small to support such a prominent and distinguished gentleman.

Duane nudged Midnight toward the lights, although he wasn't in the mood for violence. Constant throbbing pain could affect the classic fast draw. All towns of the same size appeared similar, and he could expect a stable, cantina, church, and store. If it's not Saturday night — should be peaceful.

He rode down the one and only street, where three horses were tied in front of the cantina, while a stagecoach rested alongside the stable. He steered Midnight toward the cantina, climbed down from the saddle, looked about cautiously, then limped into the ramshackle structure.

It held a table of cardplayers, a few drinkers at the bar, and a solitary bearded gentleman sitting in the corner, looking out of place. Duane made his way to the man in the apron, who filled a glass with mescal. Duane flipped him a coin, sipped fiery refreshment, wiped his mouth with the back of his hand, and said, "You don't happen to know where I can find a doctor, do you?"

The bartender pointed to the man in the corner. "You are lucky, because there is one right there. He arrived a few hours ago on the stagecoach."

Duane dragged his foot across the floor, and was dismayed to see that the medical practitioner was passed out cold, a half bottle of mescal in front of him. I don't need a drunkard, decided Duane. He was turning away, when the doctor opened his eyes. "Did you wish to speak with me, Americano?"

"I was shot in the leg," replied Duane, "and I'm afraid it's infected. Can you take a look or are you too drunk?"

"Drunk?" The doctor placed his hand on his breast. "Of course I'm not drunk. I was only resting."

A wave of alcohol fumes struck Duane in the face, but the old soak was the only assistance available. Duane pulled off his boot, then lay face down on the floor. The doctor brought the oil lamp closer, knelt beside him, brought his eye close to the wound, and said: "Hmmmm." He opened his little black bag, pulled out a pair of tweezers, and poked the instrument into the wound. "Looks all right to me. Just a matter of time till it heals. This is going to hurt." The doctor poured mescal into the wound, but no sound escaped Duane's lips. The doctor dabbed the mescal with a white cloth. "What's your name?"

"José."

"You look familiar, José. Have we ever met?"

"Not that I recall."

The doctor tied on the bandage. "Try to stay off it, and let nature take its course. Where are you from, José?"

"*Tejas.*"

"You are a desperado, no? Well, I always charge desperados more. Fifty pesos, please."

Duane paid him, then returned to the bar, relieved that he didn't need leg amputation, but not trusting the medical advice entirely. "Hit me again," he told the bartender.

"Hold it right there," said a voice behind him. "Don't move a muscle, or I'll kill you."

Duane had become distracted, permitting someone to creep up on him. The Pecos Kid tried to smile. "What's the problem, friend?"

"Hold 'em high, and if you try somethin', yer a dead son-of-a-bitch."

The man came behind Duane and pulled Duane's Colt out of its holster, then removed the knife in his boot. "You can turn around, but do it real slow, and don't make no fast moves."

Duane saw a tall blond gringo standing in front of him, holding a gun aimed at his chest. "I guess you don't reckernize me, but we run into each other in Zumarraga. I couldn't get into position fast enough, then you left town. There's a five-hundred-dollar reward on yer ass, and I'm a-gonna claim it." The bounty hunter reached into his pocket and took out a wanted picture with Duane's sketched unshaven face on it. "Whoop dee do — looks like I'm rich!"

Duane recalled the blond gringo from Zumarraga. "I always wondered what kind of polecat would become a bounty hunter."

"Just walk to yer horse, Mister Pecos. And no funny moves, if'n you don't mind."

Duane wondered if there was a trick or ruse he could use to escape. Naked before a loaded gun, he knew it wouldn't be easy, but he'd rather die than get locked in a cell.

"I'm a-gonna tie you up," said the bounty hunter. "Lie down whar you are, put yer hands behind yer back, and don't make no funny moves, cause I'll pop you right in the ear."

"I'd like to know your name," said Duane.

"None of yer fuckin' business. Git down and do what I say."

It was bare ground in front of the cantina, covered with gobs of spit, cigarette butts, and a splash of something that looked like vomit. Stark desperation assailed Duane as he lowered himself to the ground. The bounty hunter bent to slip a hitch over one wrist, and the Pecos Kid knew it was now or never. In a sudden Apache explosion of muscles and sinews, he was up and spinning, grabbing for the bounty hunter's gun hand.

The gun fired, its flash blinding Duane, and the ground blasted three inches from his left ear. The bounty hunter was knocked off his feet, then Duane twisted the gun out of his hand, turned the barrel swiftly, and aimed it at the bounty hunter's nose.

The bounty hunter smiled nervously, showing large white teeth. "Looks like you got the drop on me."

"Hand me my gun real slow, butt first."

The bounty hunter took the gun by the barrel and held it out to Duane. "Guess yer as rough as they say, Mister Braddock."

"Guess I am."

Duane couldn't shoot him in cold blood, but didn't want a bounty hunter on his trail. "Listen to me carefully," said Duane. "I've killed to defend my life, and I'll kill you too, Mister Bounty Hunter Man, if I ever see you crawling up on me again."

The bounty hunter bravely tried to smile. "Yes sir."

"Stand in the middle of the street, and don't get funny on me. You give me a reason — I'll blow your damned fool head off."

The bounty hunter obeyed orders as Duane aimed his Colt at him. Duane climbed into the saddle, backed Midnight into the street, and rode toward the bounty hunter, still levelling the gun. Midnight stopped in front of the bounty hunter, and Duane said, "Nobody's ever going to lock me up, and you can tell that to any lawman. If you ever see me again, you'd better start running. Got me?"

The bounty hunter nodded solemnly, as he gazed down the barrel of the most profound argument in the world. "Yes sir."

Duane pulled Midnight's reins to the side, and Midnight raised his front hooves high in the air. Then he turned, Duane gave him some spur, and the horse broke into a gallop, carrying the Pecos Kid swiftly into the night.

The bounty hunter stood in the middle of the street, watching horse and rider disappear. Then he sighed in relief, shook out his arms, and returned to the cantina.

All eyes were on him as he approached the bartender, who filled a glass without being asked. The bounty hunter's name was Hank Grimble, and he gulped the contents down. Then he placed the glass on the bar, and said, "That was too close for comfort."

The bartender nodded in agreement. "I wonder who he was?"

"In Texas, we call him the Pecos Kid. He's supposed to be one bad *hombre,* and I guess that's so."

"You owe your life to him, señor. If it had been me — I would have killed you."

The bartender filled another glass, and Grimble's hand trembled as he carried it to a table against the wall. He sat, stared into space, and tried to understand what happened. One moment he'd had the Pecos Kid pinned, and the next he was looking at the business end of a Colt .44. He'd heard stories about the Kid's uncanny speed, but figured it was the usual exaggeration. The bounty hunter took off his cowboy hat and wiped his forehead with the back of his sleeve. *Maybe it's time I found another line of work.*

Duane rode all night, slept the next day, and hit the trail at sundown. He continued this schedule for the next several days, as he advanced toward his native land.

In dreams, he held Doña Consuelo in his arms, but he awakened to find himself alone, with flies buzzing his nose. He maintained a constant watch on his back trail, in case a certain blond head turned up unexpectedly. His behavior was furtive, secretive, and ready for anything. He slept with his Colt loaded but uncocked in his right hand.

Sometimes, drowsing in the saddle, he recalled his all-too-brief weeks with Doña Consuelo de Rebozo. The longing refused to depart, and he realized that he cared for the Spanish noblewoman deeply. *Someday we'll be together again, my darling,* he swore, while another part of his mind wondered if he'd ever see her again.

The closer he drew to the Rio Grande,

the more he found himself thinking about America. I'll change my name, and become just another cowboy drifter fool. Nobody'll notice me if I stay out of trouble, but when have I ever stayed out of trouble?

One night, he stopped at a water hole surrounded by green oaks, cottonwoods, and swales of grass. He knew that such tempting sites were the most dangerous places for white eyes, but it was dark, and he wasn't expected. He stopped Midnight, listened, and asked, "What do you think, feller?"

Midnight twitched his ear. Looks okay to me, pard.

They'd been getting along better, as they'd spent more time together. Duane dismounted, led Midnight to the water, loosened the cinches, and then filled the canteens. Next, the fugitive took off his hat, thrust his head beneath the surface, and raised it swiftly. Dripping wet, he tied canteens to the saddles, checked Midnight's hooves, and made sure nothing was chafing the animal's hide. He was about to climb back into the saddle, when he noted a poster nailed to a nearby tree.

Wouldn't it be a kick in the ass if that's my face over there? he asked himself, as he led Midnight toward the document. But after several more steps he noticed that nobody's image had been drawn on the poster. Instead, it consisted of the following message:

Appearing nightly
the famous, one and only
MISS VANESSA FONTAINE
"The Charleston Nightingale"
Last Chance Saloon
Escondido, Texas

CHAPTER 13

Maggie O'Day looked up from her desk, as the door opened. It was Miss Vanessa Fontaine, fifteen minutes before her next performance. "I've reached a decision," said the Charleston Nightingale. "This is my last week."

Maggie puffed her cigar skeptically. "That's what you say every Monday."

Vanessa sat on the chair, her back ramrod-straight. "I'm at the point where I'm losing respect for myself, so I'm taking the next stage east — sorry. If Duane Braddock shows up after I've gone, tell him I'm in Charleston. If I'm going to be a singer, I might as well get serious about it. I think I'm ready for concert halls."

"I agree — you've got too much talent fer this li'l border town," replied Maggie, "but yer still a woman in love, and I don't believe yer a-goin' nowheres."

Vanessa narrowed her eyes with determination. "I'll never stop loving him, but I'm so sick of Escondido — I'm ready to scream."

"This town's sure ain't got much," Maggie agreed. "I'd be a damned fool if I said otherwise, and I plan to leave myself someday, but one of these nights — I can feel it in my bones — young Duane is a-gonna show up. Hell, he's long overdue, and it might even be tonight."

There was a knock on the door. "Time to make the announcements, Miss O'Day."

Maggie strode toward the saloon, pushed through the crowd, and climbed onto the stage. Then she launched her introduction, while Vanessa waited in the shadows, hoping that Duane would be there, but it was always the same, and she was tired of letdowns. I've never been so unhappy in all my days, she confessed to herself. The only thing to do is hit the trail, otherwise I'll go mad in this ratty little border town.

She heard Maggie speak her name, and the saloon echoed with outbursts of joy and expectation. Miss Vanessa Fontaine squared her shoulders, went up on her toes, and advanced theatrically toward the stage, as a wide path of admirers opened for her. They winked, smiled, licked their chops, drooled, burped. Some had eyes like saucers traced with red ink. She landed on the stage, bowed, and scanned their faces, looking for *him* amid peals of homage and praise. But he wasn't there, as usual, so all she could do was quiet them down, make her usual preliminary remarks, and after they were properly quiet, she placed one palm in the other, and performed:

> *"Way down upon the Swanee River*
> *Far, far away,*
> *That's where my heart is turning ever,*
> *There's where the old folks stay . . ."*

Her voice wafted across the saloon as she drew them skillfully into her fantasy web. She knew which songs calmed them, and what pepped them up, playing an audience like a virtuoso violinist. Then, during the chorus, she spotted a certain tall, bearded cowboy wearing a black hat with a silver concho hatband standing near the bar. Her voice caught in her throat momentarily, but she recovered quickly, and the polished performer continued the final stanza:

*"All the world is sad and dreary
everywhere I roam;
oh, darkeys, how my heart grows weary,
far from the old folks at home."*

Vanessa felt faint as she took her first bow. It can't be, she told herself. She brought herself to full height, and glanced toward the bar, but the cowboy was gone. This damned town and all that mescal are driving me loco.

Coins rained onto the stage, a stagecoach driver hooted, a cowboy whistled, and somebody threw an empty bottle of mescal into the fireplace. Vanessa bowed again, then waited patiently for them to simmer down. Lots of cowboys wear beards, she told herself, and you can buy a silver concho hatband anywhere. The applause diminished, she filled her lungs with air, and began her next selection:

*"Many are the hearts that are weary tonight,
Wishing for the war to cease
Many are the hearts that are looking for
     the right
To see the dawn of peace."*

She liked to look every patron in the eye, because she wanted them to know that she was searching too. Then, against the right wall, she spotted a pair of green almond orbs beneath the same silver concho hatband. It was the bearded young man again, a glass in his hand and a half-smile on his face. Her mind subtracted the beard, she glanced at his shoulders, and realized that she was looking at her former fiancé, the notorious Pecos Kid!

Other patrons were glancing at their ex-sheriff, although Miss Vanessa Fontaine was supposed to be center of attention. The Kid stood confidently, resting his right hand on his Colt .44. I wonder if he's here to kill me! she thought, as she sang:

> *"We've been tenting tonight*
>   *on the cold camp ground,*
> *Thinking of days gone by,*
> *Of the loved ones at home who*
>   *gave us a hand,*
> *And the tear that said 'Goodbye.'"*

She came to the end of her song, took her bow, and the rafters trembled with ovations, but when she raised her head, the Pecos Kid was gone. She followed the attention of her audience, and now he sat at a table with his back against the wall, and his eyes spiked into her brain. Vanessa smiled gaily, and said: "I'd like to dedicate my next song to an old friend. I wronged him once, and I pray that someday he'll forgive me." She raised her arms, and sang:

"The same canteen, my soldier friend,
The same canteen, I say
There's never a bond, old friend, like this —
We have drunk from the same canteen."

The saloon was silent, except for her lilting voice. Duane feasted his eyes upon her, as he relived the pleasurable pain of his romance with Miss Vanessa Fontaine. He'd already spoken with the bartender, who'd told him that she'd become a widow, and more importantly, hadn't been with any men in Escondido. Why is she here? Duane asked himself. She hasn't been following me, has she?

It was difficult for him to believe, because he knew how selfish and disdainful was Miss Vanessa Fontaine. But what other reason would bring her to Escondido? His rapturous nights with Doña Consuelo faded in his mind as he gazed upon tall, slim, golden-tressed Miss Vanessa Fontaine, the woman of his dreams, performing onstage at the

Last Chance Saloon.

"It was sometimes water, and
  sometimes, milk,
Sometimes applejack, fine as silk
but whatever the tipple has been,
We shared it together, in bane or bliss,
We have drunk from the same canteen."

She paused at the end of the song, and
the saloon was so quiet the breeze could be
heard against windows. Then she touched
her fingers to her lips, blew Duane a kiss,
and bowed.

The saloon burst with tumultuous hur-
rahs, because everyone had shared a drink
with a friend or lover, and Vanessa knew
well how to set the scene. Even the Pecos
Kid was on his feet, clapping hands enthu-
siastically, trying to whistle between his
teeth like a cowboy, but failing miserably.

I've been dreaming about that long tall
sally ever since I met her, he told himself,
and tonight she'll be mine. At that
moment, on the very pinnacle of exulta-
tion, he felt something cold and metallic
press behind his left ear, as a voice said
harshly: "Move a muscle, and yer dead!"

Duane froze, his heart nearly stopped,
and he realized with sinking heart that he'd

relaxed at the wrong moment yet again. Miss Vanessa Fontaine was staring at him with her mouth hanging open, and all eyes turned toward the strange scene unfolding against the wall.

"Raise your hands," said ex-sheriff J. T. Sturgis, crouching and aiming his Remington at the Pecos Kid.

All Duane could do was reach for the ceiling. The veteran of Pickett's Charge took the fugitive's Colt and Apache knife. "Turn around real slow."

Duane eased toward a man with a solid jaw, mustache, round nose, and steely gaze. "My name's J. T. Sturgis, and yer under arrest fer the murder of Saul Klevins, Otis Puckett, Jay Krenshaw, and the Devil's Creek Massacre. You give me the least bit of trouble, I'll shoot you where you stand."

A commotion broke out nearby, forcing Sturgis to take his eyes off Duane for a critical moment. Patrons were drawing their guns, and even Miss Vanessa Fontaine had her faithful derringer in her hand, while Maggie O'Day came at Sturgis from the right with a sawed-off shotgun in her hands. The next thing Sturgis knew, something grabbed his throat, and a powerful force slammed him to the floor, knocking the wind out of him. When he opened his eyes, he saw the barrel of a Colt pointed at his nose, and the face of the Pecos Kid hovered above him. "Who the fuck are you?"

Maggie explained: "That's J. T. Sturgis, and he used to be sheriff hyar. But I fired him, and now he wants the bounty on yer head, Kid."

Sturgis looked up at Duane. "There's warrants fer yer arrest all over this territory, but I'm the only person in Escondido who believes in the law."

"I ought to kill you," replied Duane, "but instead I'll have to lock you up."

"Go ahead," snarled Sturgis, "but I'll git out someday, and I'll foller you to the end of the earth, 'cause somebody has to bring you before the bar of justice."

"I'd rather go before the bar of this saloon," Duane replied. "Why don't you let me buy you a drink?"

"You don't charm me, Mister Pecos Kid. I know all about the Devil's Creek Massacre, and a few other things."

"I was at the Massacre," allowed Duane, "but I was a prisoner of the outlaws, and didn't have anything to do with it. I guess you don't believe me."

"Yer damned right I don't, because I knows a killer when I sees one. Yer baby eyes don't fool me one bit." Sturgis balled his fists as he glowered at Maggie O'Day, Vanessa Fontaine, and the audience at the Last Chance Saloon. "If you don't help me, it makes all of you accomplices. If anything happens to me, you'll have a lot to answer fer."

Maggie roared: "This son-of-a-bitch wants to hang everybody in sight! He thinks he knows what's right, and everybody else is wrong!"

Duane aimed his Colt at Sturgis. "Get going."

Sturgis headed for the door, his face red with frustration and embarrassment. He'd been defeated once more, and felt the compelling need to redeem his failed life. Desperate, humiliated, he noticed an old drunkard standing in his path, a cocked gun in his hand, apparently on the verge of passing out. A remote chance beckoned, and perhaps if Corporal Sturgis had continued to charge Cemetery Ridge, he might've led the old 9th Virginia to the summit, and turned the tide at Gettysburg. Isn't life made of chances and small turns of fate? he asked himself, as he lunged for the revolver.

Duane hollered: "Don't!"

But Sturgis was already in motion,

swinging the revolver around. All Duane could do was open fire at point-blank range, and the saloon filled with the judgment of Colonel Colt. One bullet struck Sturgis in the chest, another smacked him in the mouth, and he was dead before he hit the floor.

Duane stood like a statue with the gun aimed straight ahead, hat low over his eyes, smoke arising from his Colt .44. Nobody dared say a word. Then Maggie O'Day stepped forward, the double-barreled shotgun in her hands. "Welcome home, Kid. It's been a long time."

The notorious outlaw cocked an eye, as he holstered his gun. "I need a drink."

"Foller me."

Duane turned toward Vanessa. "Is your show over?"

"It is now."

Duane remained poised for danger, but saw admiration, awe, and the morbid fascination of crowds as he made his way toward the corridor. Maggie opened the door of her office, and Duane sat beside Vanessa in front of the desk. The Pecos Kid turned toward his former lady love and said: "How're you doing?"

"My late husband has left me a small fortune."

"What're you going to do with it?"

"Spend it on you."

Maggie settled her ruffled skirts behind the desk and shook her head with dismay. "Just like a woman, give everything she's got to a man, and you can't trust 'em as far as you can throw the Last Chance Saloon."

"But I didn't leave her," explained Duane. "She's the one who left me."

"I made a mistake," Vanessa replied, "but maybe I needed to be apart from you, to realize how much I really needed you."

Duane looked her in the eye. "I wouldn't trust you as far as I can throw the Last Chance Saloon."

Vanessa noticed a new maturity and confidence in him, and he appeared a dangerous rascal in a beard, except for his beautifully formed nose, red lips, and those overwhelming eyes. "You're not trying to tell me that you've been pure since you've last seen me, Duane Braddock."

He couldn't lie, but a blush came over his face.

"Just as I thought," said Vanessa. "He's been screwing his way across Mexico."

Maggie puffed her cigar. "Neither one of us is an angel here, so let's cut the horseshit." She looked at Duane. "What's up?"

"Is the cavalry in the area, by any chance?"

Maggie shook her head. "The only law in this town is you, if you want yer old job back."

"No, thanks, because I'm on my way to the Pecos Country."

Maggie and Vanessa glanced at each other, because both knew the import of that remark. Duane intended to avenge the murder of his parents, kill or be killed, winner take all.

"I don't suppose there's anything I can say to change yer mind," said Maggie, "so let's have that drink."

She pulled a bottle and three glasses out of the bottom drawer, poured, and said, "Here's to the Pecos Kid."

They touched glasses as the door opened. One of the waitresses stuck her head inside. "Bartender wants to talk with you, Miss O'Day."

Maggie left the office, and the two ex-lovers were alone for the first time since Vanessa had told Duane that she was marrying another man. "Do you hate me very much?" asked the former Charleston belle.

"I don't hate you at all, and as a matter of fact, I've never been able to forget you."

His words were a balm on her heart, and

she found herself sitting on his lap. "We were so poor, I couldn't bear it any more," she explained.

"Sounds like money isn't a problem anymore. After I'm finished in the Pecos Country, we'll tie the knot."

"*If* you return," she reminded him. "I'll bet there's a telegram on the way to Mister Archer even as we speak, telling him you're in Escondido."

"In my line of work, it's best to stay in motion."

"Not without me."

"You'd better think it over, Vanessa. It might get hotter'n hell in Edgeville."

"I'm not letting you get away a second time, after all the trouble I went through to find you. Besides, it's always best to travel with a woman, because a woman makes a man appear legitimate. They're expecting a vagabond cowboy called the Pecos Kid, not a well-dressed businessman with his elegant, cultivated wife."

Duane was thrilled by the feel of her tall figure in his lap, and he couldn't keep his hands off those long scrumptious legs. "Is there anyplace where we can be alone?"

"My room is down the hall."

They made their way through the labyrinth, passing cowboys and prostitutes also

341

on amorous rounds, and finally ended at the door of Miss Vanessa Fontaine. She unlocked it, and he reached for her arm before she could light the lamp. She turned toward him, their lips brushed, and then his hands were all over her, as small sounds emitted from her throat.

With trembling hands, the lovers undressed in pale light streaming through the window. He caught a glimpse of her tall, white elegance disappearing beneath the covers of the big brass bed, and seconds later he was with her.

Their bare bodies touched, and the artery in his throat throbbed as her familiar svelte configuration melted into his. They rolled over the bedspread, bruising each other's lips with reckless passion. Finally he held her beneath him, gazed into her eyes, and said, "I've dreamed of this moment, but never thought it'd really happen."

"I wondered if I was chasing a fantasy, but I prayed every night, and here you are."

They embraced in the darkness, their bodies became one, and the bed muttered a silent protest, as coyotes howled mournfully in the Sierra Madre mountains, and Midnight drowsed at the rail in front of the

Last Chance Saloon.

The great black beast knew that his boss had forgotten him again, but his lot was no different from any other mount in Escondido, and at least he had a trough of clear water. I'd better rest while I have the chance, thought he. Crazy two-legged son-of-a-bitch always lands in trouble, and he'll probably get me killed one of these days.

The melancholy Hamlet of horses dozed fitfully, as stars glittered above the little town of Escondido. Laughter erupted at the bar of the Last Chance Saloon, where a cowboy at a nearby table won the next deal, while across the backyard, a few hundred yards away, J. T. Sturgis lay naked on a cold slab in the undertaker's office.

The room was dark, for the undertaker was enjoying certain acrobatic acts in a bedroom behind the Last Chance Saloon. Sturgis hadn't been bathed or undressed, and appeared as when he'd fallen, with the same expression of wonderment and relief on his distorted features. Here lies a brave soldier who died in pursuit of his duties, as he saw them in his heart. The moon shone impartially on death, love, and lost illusions, as Texas spiraled through the cosmos, heading toward a bright new morning.